Aliens in the Soda Machine and Other Strange Tales

By Reggie Lutz

I0521229

Text copyright © 2015 Reggie Lutz

All Rights Reserved

Disclaimer: Herein lie works of fiction. Any resemblance to persons, living or dead, and events is coincidental.

One-Hundred Eye Curse originally appeared in Greek Myths Revisited, 2011, Wicked East Press

Ewe Bluhdprat and the All-Knowing Gargoyle originally appeared in Don't Tread on Me: Tales of Revenge and Retribution, 2010, Static Movement

Ice Masons originally appeared in Best New Writing 2008, 2008, Hopewell Publications

Fork You – A Gladiola Johnson Story (For Proserpine) originally appeared in Panverse One, 2009, Panverse Publishing

4

Contents

INTRODUCTION by Dario Ciriello

I first encountered Reggie Lutz's work in 2009, while collecting stories for my novella anthology, *Panverse One*. Sifting through submissions, as any editor will tell you, is like looking for a diamond in a coal mine. You read a lot of work that ranges from the indifferent to the downright awful; your eyes begin to glaze over, and you wonder why you ever got into this game. You feel yourself losing the will to live… and then you see a brilliant gleam of pure white light in the suffocating darkness. Somewhere, angels sing.

That's how I felt on first reading Reggie's story, *Fork You*. She had me at the first lines, and I soon found myself immersed in the richly-imagined, highly improbable world of wild child Gladiola Johnson. Who was this writer? Why hadn't I come across her work before?

I bought the story, the anthology was published to good reviews, Reggie's piece turned out to be a favorite among readers, and Reggie kept on writing.

And now, this collection.

If you're new to Reggie's work, you're in for a treat. Reggie has an eye for the oddball, the misfit. Her characters are driven by weird forces, their lives and surroundings densely textured and meticulously observed. Her story worlds are our world, but tinged with the surreal, and underpinned with the eldritch, sometimes claustrophobic, logic of dream.

The work in this collection is hard to categorize; although bordering on urban fantasy, new weird, and interstitial, in the end I would have to call it literary for its themes, its sensibilities, and the occasional, often startling flash of soaring language that bursts from Reggie's direct, easy prose.

Aliens in the Soda Machine is a collection to be read slowly, one story at a time. Each piece needs space, time, and consideration. And long after you're finished, don't be surprised if stray images and resonant echoes from Reggie's stories burst from your subconscious when you least expect it.

-- Pasadena, CA, February 2015

Ice Masons

The storm windows on the front porch barely kept out the Pennsylvania winter chill. A high temperature of five degrees. Ridiculous even for mid-winter.

Ruth watched puffs of her breath crystallize in the air, mingling with the smoke from her cigarette as she exhaled. "Exhalations in exile," she muttered to herself. There was no one to take care of in the tiny one-bedroom house, which was more like a cottage. The cat had run away a few days ago, though every time Ruth ran the vacuum cleaner, it kicked up reminders of the cat's existence: hair balls, tiny bright shredded material from cat toys, pieces of hard cat food that hid inside barely perceptible crevices.

Ruth felt as if she had spent centuries alone in the house, though it had only been a week. Seven days since Philip had died, leaving her nothing but this tiny house on the edge of what used to be a working farm. In winter, it was sometimes impossible to leave. When Phil had been alive, it was cozy, fun. They'd laugh, play board games, shovel snow, watch classic movies on cable, drink hot cocoa, and smoke on the enclosed porch, taking drags from each other's cigarettes, moaning about how they should quit.

"It's us against a hostile world, babe," Phil smirked. And Ruth would answer, "Better get the shotgun out, honey," or "Batten down the hatches!" with laughter in her voice. The world did not seem hostile to her with Phil at her side, keeping everything warm with his humor, the light in his eyes, the huge body that sheltered her at night when the howling winter wind threatened to blow their little cottage away. Now that Phil was gone, it was easy to remember the good times, idealize the past. Maybe too easy.

Just one week ago, snow had seemed magical, the woods enchanted by ice fairies whose job it was to delight them by encrusting the trees with diamonds of water. Ruth had made an attempt to capture that magic with paint, with film, and she'd come close once or twice.

She and Philip had not been extremely wealthy, but they did well enough working for themselves, she an artist, he a computer programmer.

Their work area was larger than the cottage that was their home. Phil had renovated the abandoned barn on the edge of the property. It was done in secret, when Ruth was still taking photography jobs that took her away for weeks at a time. He'd installed a skylight in the roof for good light in which to paint, and built a darkroom. Ruth had been stunned and thrilled when he'd presented it to her as a gift for their one-year anniversary.

Her big gift to him that year was a deadline for herself to give up work in the city. She'd bought him a leather winter coat and boots, and a pearl-handled hunting knife. Inside the coat, she'd placed a black and white photo of downed tree branches used to spell out the date, a shot that had taken her hours to compose.

Ruth sighed, pressed her forehead against the screen, and the glass of the storm window beyond that, the wires of the screen biting into her skin as the smooth glass cooled.

Her agent was already plaguing her with phone calls.

"Come back to New York. You need to think about your future, your career."

Ruth hearing her own voice in response, as if it were on a distant island and not coming out of her own head. "I don't know. It's too soon." Calm, when inside she was still howling—a beast wanted to reach through the phone lines and strangle the pushy agent.

Well, honey, take whatever time you need, but not too much time. Life is waiting here for you—followed by the litany of offers from ad agencies, magazines, publishers who needed book covers—*It can't wait forever, you know*—and Ruth barely hearing what the agent had to say, cutting her off—*I have to go.* Tears began before the receiver hit the cradle. Not ready to think about a life without Phil.

There had been no warning, no wasting disease, no tumors or diabetes or ebola virus. His death was as sudden as an accidental beam of refracted light spoiling a perfect shot. One minute, Phil was grinning his grizzly bear smile through the brown and gray beard he grew only in winter, waving good bye and blowing kisses. In the next moment, he was crushed inside his Toyota, which was flattened between a semi and a stone wall. Dead before the Jaws of Life arrived to pry him out.

Scenes of that day rolled by on the vast blanket of white snow that stretched out in front of the cottage. Ruth on her way home from the grocery store slowing at the scene of an accident, a sick feeling in her stomach. A barely recognizable car crushed against stone, a hardly scratched semi-truck parked on the opposite side of the road. Tire marks, the smell of burnt rubber, chemical combustion. Ruth, seeing the greenish-gray paint of the Toyota in flecks on the asphalt. She who hated gawkers and nosy neighbors, not wanting to stop, but stopping anyway, knowing before she asked yet still pulling over to the side of the road, up to the policeman directing nonexistent traffic. She could see the expression on his face through the windshield as she slowed, the officer preparing to tell her to "move along please, there's nothing to see here." Ruth knowing that something in her face must have caused his expression to soften, the officer's eyes to grow wide, eyes the same gold-flecked green as Phil's. Ruth, watching the officer's adam's apple bobbing up and down, unable to look at the green of his eyes. The officer, stared, swallowed; asked, before she had a chance to open her mouth, "I'm sorry ma'am, but is your last name Mason?"

"Yes."

"Your husband is Phil Mason?"

A nod. A brief moment of guilty relief. Then silent tears streaming down her face as Ruth could swear she felt Phil's breath on her neck, a kiss goodbye, leaving her to stare at the ruined car, the flecks of paint and smoking car parts on the road, the license plate twisted, but still identifiable, though her husband's body was not. Phil reduced to a violent mash of human pigment on the canvas of asphalt.

***

Phil had no family so there was no one to help Ruth with the funeral arrangements; wake, service, casket, announcements, calling the friends, those who had hired Phil, the insurance company. Ruth's family consisted of an older sister, Amanda, a "free spirit" who was in New Zealand with her lover. She was unable to make it back to the States in time for the funeral, but she had offered to fly back as soon as she could, to stay with Ruth for a while, to help her get back on track with her life. It was as if Ruth's agent, Lori and Amanda were conspiring to get her out of the cottage, back to her old life, though they had never spoken to each other as far as Ruth knew.

On the phone, Ruth insisted, "No. There's more than enough to keep me busy. Don't worry."

"I don't like how you sound."

"Amanda, my husband just died. Of course I sound strange. And you're on the other side of the world."

"But you're all alone in the middle of the woods."

"There's Kitten."

"I thought you said Kitten ran away?"

"She'll be back," and Ruth knew it wasn't true, but she couldn't imagine her breezy, colorful sister in her cottage, where she and Phil had built their quiet life together. Amanda would describe it as boring, making the sanctuary less of a haven with derision.

A beat of static silence, Amanda's sharp tone of irritation, calling, "Ruth."

"What?"

"I'm not going to insist. Are you sure you want to go through this alone? Are you sure you won't be mad at me later?"

Ruth sighed, feeling older than her older sibling, more ancient than the first cave painting, and so tired. "I'm sure. I want to be alone with my memories of him for a while."

Ruth could feel her sister's tension through the phone lines. "Okay Ruthie, but I'm calling you every day until you do something with yourself, until you're out of the woods."

Ruth wanted to protest that she wasn't in the midst of some dark fairy tale forest, with ogres hiding behind every tree and no knights to call to for help. She wanted to explain that she was not going to waste away into oblivion even though she sometimes felt like doing that, like joining Phil. Phil, who had been her knight in a fuzzy sweater, blue jeans and boots, long johns underneath to keep him warm. "My winter uniform," he'd say with a laugh, when he pulled them on in the morning or tugged them off at night.

The winter uniform was what Ruth had chosen for him to wear at the wake. She knew that his friends, the chosen family would see the choice as strange. "It was what he was happiest wearing. He hated suits."

The contrast between them as a couple must have been odd to outsiders, Ruth thought. She preferred to wear long, elegant lacy things, or tailored women's suits, whereas he was as much a woodsman as the hero in *Little Red Riding Hood.*

They'd met in New York. He was designing photographic software for a large company that wanted him on-site to answer questions, test the prototype, iron out glitches. Ruth had been called in to consult on the version for professionals, to point out features that would be desirable for photographers who got paid, or aspired to get paid, for their work.

It had been a chaotic time her life. Art and ads and photojournalism and fashion and parties and travel and schmoozing. Everything was a constant struggle to get her name out there, to be seen, her unique vision paid for so she could live her dream of being an artist. She thought herself happy, but the face looking back at her in the mirror each morning told her a different story. She had the look of a hunted animal. Even as Ruth stalked success she was depleted by its demands. What Ruth desired was the freedom to create, not the gritty glamour of crowds.

When she met Phil, she loved his calm, loved how he stuck out from the crowd of city hipsters, conspicuously uncool and not caring. One night, when Ruth was aching for a tranquil night alone, she had to attend a company dinner. She could opt out, there was always a choice, but Lori strong-armed her into going, reminding her that, "this is how the next job is landed, how positive reputations are formed." Ruth rolled her eyes, acquiesced, and decided to make the best of it.

The restaurant was a posh new place, elegantly decorated with cherry-stained wood, dark green paint, brass fixtures, and candlelight. Exactly the kind of safe hip that Ruth had lately begun to associate with the New York scene. The dinner party was also tastefully decorated, in cool New York black. Amid the herd of darkly-clad New Yorkers, it was a shock to see a tall, bearded man wearing a bright red sweater, like a yule-tide poinsettia at a funeral. His blue jeans were so new the hue of them screamed. The beard, in a tundra of clean-shaven faces, was a promise of new, unfettered growth. Ruth swore she could smell woodland pine trees in the air. At her shoulder, Lori shuddered, "My god. What a hick."

Ruth shrugged, annoyed at the comment. She could not take her eyes off him. He laughed at something said by a bland suit, his smile easy, his posture relaxed. He caught her eye and dazzled her with his smile. Ruth smiled back. To her agent she said, "I don't think so. I think he's refreshing."

Lori blinked. "Well, you are the artist. You see things I don't."

A few moments later, Ruth found herself seated next to him. She was distracted by his woodland smell, rendered unable to follow the fast-paced banter that ping-ponged around the table. Still, she couldn't bring herself to break in and talk to him. Then, between dinner and desert, Phil interrupted a conversation about the Hiltons to ask if there was somewhere he could smoke.

"There's a patio in the back," said Lori.

Phil gently nudged Ruth's shoulder and asked, "Would you like to join me?"

"I would love to," Ruth murmured.

"I hope you don't think this is out of line," Phil began as he opened the door for her, "but I thought you looked kind of bored in there."

It was an open invitation to unload her burden of discontent and Ruth took it. He nodded in all the right places, said nothing derisive; he didn't even give her the lecture she usually heard, which was that now was the time to pay her dues, that she could rest later. He made all the right attentive noises. Ruth did not have time to extend the same courtesy to Phil. Lori came to retrieve them for coffee, and they didn't talk for the rest of the night.

When she got home, she couldn't sleep, agonizing about what she'd said, whom he might repeat it to, what he must think of her whining. She was certain he would never want to see her again.

But then he called her the next day for lunch.

Over the following weeks she spent every spare moment she could with Phil. She loved his enthusiasm for new things and how comfortable he was in his skin. Through the lens of Phil, she looked at the city with new eyes. The first time he was in her tiny apartment, he didn't seem to notice the cracks in the walls, the noise of the neighbors fighting; he'd walked straight to her window and said, "Ruth, this is beautiful."

She joined him at the window and looked out at the lights across the city. Standing beside him, she felt her anxiety melt. He put his arm around her and it made her feel safe, protected. She breathed in the scent of him, and sound faded. She didn't want to speak and spoil the moment, and was almost disappointed when he did.

"If you really look," Phil whispered, "It's like a giant forest, it glitters like ice-covered trees in winter."

She looked out and for a moment she could see the forest and the city superimposed on each other, like a double exposure. The sound of snow crunching underfoot. The sound of trees creaking under the weight of ice, and the air smelling clean. The moment was ethereal: Phil was magic. She turned to look in his eyes, saw the wood reflected there, and kissed him.

When she turned back to the view, the wood was gone; her sleep deprivation washed over her and she began to cry.

"Ruth, what's wrong?"

"I'm just so tired."

She sobbed into his sweater, hating herself for feeling so weak, so frustrated. She wanted to be happy, not lean so hard on him. "I hate being like this. I'm sorry."

"Sh. Don't apologize," he said, stroking her hair.

Ruth melted into him, not a person but a malleable blob, and all the energy of her sorrow leeched into him. Just before she fell asleep in his arms she muttered, "Take me away from all of this!"

He said, "I will."

They married the next day at the Justice of the Peace and spent the honeymoon packing. In a month they'd moved to the cottage in the woods of Pennsylvania, or Pennsyltucky as her agent called it. She didn't care what Lori thought— she was happy, building a new life, a new family, with Phil and Kitten the cat.

It turned out that Phil sometimes had to travel for work. Ruth did not mind. After the crazy, crowded days and nights of the city, she reveled in solitude. She worked, building a portfolio as thick as the Oxford English Dictionary; and when Phil came home, she had all of herself to give to him. She, the cosmopolitan hermit, he a woodland creature returning home from an adventure in the city.

One morning, before Phil had to leave again, he asked, "Ruth are you sure you're happy here? That this is what you want?"

Ruth laughed, "I haven't felt this good since I was a teenager. Yes, this is what I want. Our life here is perfect."

He leaned over the table to kiss her. "I could get used to having you here all to myself. My own woodland princess."

"I'm your ice princess, babe," Ruth replied, "You're the only one who can thaw me out."

He wriggled his eyebrows comically. "Just wait until I get back."

Ruth and Phil Mason had only three years together as a couple. She didn't want to remember the bad parts of her marriage. She was as in love with the ideal version of their union as she had been with him. Tension was new territory, discovered only six months before Phil's death, when he came home from a long trip and surprised her with the declaration, "No more business trips, Ruthie. It's all set up. I can stay here and telecommute, and we can start a family."

He'd brought roses, hiding his face behind them when he came to the front door, knocking as if courting her rather than returning to his own home. Ceremoniously, he handed her a rectangular box wrapped in red shiny paper and lace; inside was a red satin nightgown and, nestled amid more rose petals, a cheap plush miniature Teddy bear declared, "I love you," via a heart shaped patch on its belly. Phil called Ruth his princess and made love to her with fierce abandon on the floor of the foyer, not waiting for the satin nightgown, or for a shower after the long journey home. The roses fell, scattered on the floor beneath her, thorns pricked her, and she barely perceived the tiny perforations in her skin, lost in the moment, carried away by Phil's joy.

She had thought she was happy.

Later, inspecting herself in the bathroom while Phil snored on the couch, she found red angry scratches on the backs of her thighs and buttocks from the thorny roses. She felt apprehensive, doubtful, as she realized that she enjoyed missing him. It made her feel guilty, so she tried to convince herself that she liked the idea of his telecommuting as much as he did.

It did not take long for once-endearing quirks to become petty annoyances.

Some mornings, Ruth did not want to wake up to see Phil's socks and underwear, soggy and wilted on the bathroom floor, and tufts of shaven beard scattered in the sink. There were evenings that she did not want to be interrupted in the middle of painting a new piece or working in the darkroom for a slow, candlelit dinner. Her irritation and guilt over feeling this way grew in proportion to each other, and still she attempted to act happy. He seemed blissfully ignorant, and this annoyed her even further. How could he not know her better than this? How could he not tell that she needed space? Their idyllic woodland cottage began to feel more like a trap than a sanctuary.

Phil doted on her, bringing her small tokens of his affection every time they were separated for more than an hour; a gift each time he went for groceries or office supplies, or went out for a few hours with the boys. Like a cat that brings a dead mouse to the one who feeds it.

Kitten often brought dead things to Phil, dragging carcasses of tiny birds, mice, and moles into the bedroom, laying them in the center of the bed, on the pillows, so that Ruth was constantly changing and laundering sheets. They ran out of things to talk about, leaving only brief conversations about the news and the weather; but he seemed happy in spite of this, which Ruth did not understand, when the small talk felt to her like a job.

There were silences, of course, but she began to feel as if she were never alone; Phil's messes always underfoot, marking the territory when Phil himself was not there to take up the space. The small gifts he brought cluttered their small cabin, her workspace. She started to anticipate interruption every time she tried to work, waiting for the slow shuffle of his steps behind her while she set up a delicate shot or filled in the finer details of an ambitious painting. Phil was everywhere, choking her just by being ever-present; until finally she got the nerve to ask, "Honey, what do you think about moving back to the city, or even to the suburbs? I could get work and you could keep working from home. We could have a bigger place."

He had looked crestfallen; his mouth drooped into a pout. "Aren't you happy here with me? I love you. I saved you from the chaos of the city because I love you."

And Ruth was stricken, wounded by his pain and the idea that she had caused it. "I love you, too, Phil. You know that. It's just..."

"It's just what?" Phil said, cruelly mimicking her feminine tone, showing her a meanness she had never seen.

She wanted to cry but did not. She looked past him to the shelf behind his head, overcrowded with knick knacks he'd mistakenly thought would bring her pleasure, but that were simply more cold, dead things brought in to freeze her out of her space.

"Phil, it's just that we've grown so quiet. I thought if we had more going on around us..."

His face reddened and he jumped up out of his seat at the kitchen table. "You want noise? Is that it? I'll give you noise!" The rage was so sudden and strange that she did not move; she was a rabbit frozen with fear, a possum playing dead in order to avoid the real death that lay in the hands of the hunter.

Phil ran around the cottage, frantically turning on radios, the television, a blender with nothing in it, fans, although it was already cold and drafty... until so much electricity was being sucked into the house that there was a short.

Darkness. The heavy breathing of exertion from him. The rapid beat of her own panicked heart.

Ruth sat silent, unmoving. She wanted to be invisible. Tears flowed down her cheeks and her knuckles shone white where she gripped her coffee mug. Not moving though she knew she was the only target left for this stranger's rage, this stranger who was her husband. He stopped, staring at her across the kitchen table, which was not enough distance. She felt heat coming off of him in waves, saw the movement of a fist being raised and knowing that he was going to strike, whimpered like a dog. Hearing the sound coming out of her, Ruth hated herself for it. What was wrong with her that she could not act to get away from the danger? Then he whirled around, knocking the objects on the shelf to the floor. She flinched as glass shattered and wood splintered, the clatter of dead things being made more dead.

He stormed out the front door, howling at the woods like a wild thing, leaving her to stare at the broken junk that were pieces of their history, the shrine of his affection for her, now destroyed. She felt drained of everything, emptied out. The exhaustion was more palpable than anything she remembered feeling during her time in the city.

The next morning, Phil had still not returned. It was then that Ruth's self-preservation was triggered. She knew he would eventually return, and they still might be able to make things right, but how to know for sure? An alternative plan was needed, an escape route.

She picked the mess up off the floor.

She phoned her agent.

"Get me steady work. Postcards, greeting cards. Something. I need to have work."

"Ruth, I thought you hated that idea. You said it was work for hacks."

"I still do, but it doesn't matter. I need the money. And Phil can't know about this."

Lori's voice over the phone was a muddled mix of concern and happiness. "I'm happy to get you work, but is everything okay? Are you in some kind of trouble? Did Phil do something?"

"No. I just need to do this."

Silence from Lori, then a deep breath. "Jesus Christ, Ruth. If something's wrong you need to tell me."

Ruth knew she was caught, but still did not want to admit that she might be in trouble. "I said nothing's wrong."

Lori, on the other end quickly responded. "Okay. I'll see what I can set up for you."

***

Phil returned two days later stinking of alcohol and sweat. He went to the bedroom without speaking to her and slept for another whole day. She sought sanctuary in the workshop and worked, communicating with Lori using Phil's phone and fax machine. She developed rolls of film that had been neglected due to his constant presence.

She heard the car pull out of the driveway and used the time to return to the cottage, to bathe, change and transfer some things to the barn in case she needed to stay there. She cleaned up after Phil, picking up the dirty clothes, making the bed, washing the dishes, then returned to her work, blocking him out of her mind.

She didn't think of him again until she heard the car pull into the driveway. Ruth did not know if he would come to get her or not, but cleaned up after herself anyway, wanting to be ready for him if he did. She was just finishing when he opened the door to the barn, snow flurries eddying around him like he was the coming storm. They stared at each other dumbly until he broke the silence.

"Come back to the house." Despite the quiet voice, it was a demand, not a request.

Ruth could not read his face, but the dark circles under his eyes told her he was tired. She noticed a smattering of gray hairs in his beard that had not been there before. Meekly, she put on her coat and followed him out into the cold, getting her feet wet in the light coating of snow that covered the path from the barn to the cottage. He walked ahead of her, without looking back.

Angry at his confidence and angry at herself, Ruth followed, just a few feet behind. *I should have made him sit down with me to talk. I should have refused to return. Why am I so silent? I wasn't like this in the city. Was I?*

He waited for her at the door, the epitome of patience. He took her coat when she entered the screened-in porch, then ushered her inside, hanging the coat on the crowded coat rack. The cottage was clean and well-ordered, which surprised her. White candles glowed in the living room and kitchen. Wine was chilling in a bucket, coffee was already brewing to be served after dinner. Chinese food was set out on the table with two place settings. A white box tied with a pink ribbon was next to her plate.

Phil silently pulled her chair out for her, and waited for her to sit. Ruth could feel him trembling behind her, his breathing shallow, as if he was physically strained. He poured the wine and served her food, then served himself and sat across the table from her. Playing host, as if she were a guest in her own home.

They sat for a few moments, listening to the wind pick up outside, letting their food get cold until he finally cleared his throat to speak.

"Ruth. I'm sorry. I don't understand what I did. I thought I was doing everything you wanted," He paused, gazing sorrowfully at her.

Ruth watched his face, eyes glowing and dark with emotional pain, as if she were a million miles away. She looked at the box and thought, *not another stupid gadget.*

"I don't," Phil started, struggling to get the words out. "I mean—"

He interrupted himself and coughed, fidgeted with his fork.

I barely know this man. Ruth wondered how she had spent nearly three years with one person without knowing him.

"What I'm trying to say, Ruth, is, can you give me some time? Can I have a few months to think about moving? I'm not easy with change."

She wanted to say no, but saw the desperation in his face and softened. She thought of the time they'd put into the relationship, into their life together, and decided that she did not want to throw all that effort away, as if it were nothing, as if it were meaningless. *We can still make it right.*

"Okay."

Phil smiled, relief flooding and brightening his face, and he seemed more like the man Ruth knew.

"I love you, Ruth."

"I love you too, Phil."

She never opened the box.

Afterwards, they lived together in a quiet, uneasy truce, until the fight started to fade. The white box and its pink ribbon was left to collect dust at the back of a kitchen cupboard because Ruth did not want to look at it. The box reminded her too much of their fight, of her own fear, her silence.

The porch now felt dead and frigid with Phil gone, in spite of the large, glowing, space heater that was cranked up to the highest setting. It didn't matter. Ruth was getting used to the cold.

She stubbed out her cigarette and hefted the white box in her hands, Phil's last gift from beyond the grave. She inhaled, holding her breath as she loosened the fading pink ribbon, closed her eyes as she lifted the lid and opened them to look at a card nestled gently in white tissue paper. "For my princess. Forgive me."

She removed the wrapped object from the box and carefully pulled off the tissue paper. Inside was an elegant shimmer, a circle of diamonds, a tiara for Phil's princess, as cold and glittery as she felt. Beneath it was a pair of plane tickets, the dates for departure and return left open.

Ruth Mason looked up at the screen, at the glass beyond it. She stared at her pale reflection and saw the New York City skyline behind it, blending with the trees.

The Call of the Morrigan

The local park had a shiny new baseball diamond. If my husband were still around he would have loved it. An old fenced-in area of grass remained where the smaller diamond used to be. It was full of debris, the most noticeable of which were beer cans. Some had probably belonged to my husband at one point. I tried not to think about that, though. He was not a pleasant drunk.

No one bothered to remove the deteriorating fence or the trash. It sat right in the middle of the park, a sepia-toned area in the center of colorful new objects. This is where the crows dropped dead out of the sky.

No satisfying answers surfaced to say what killed them. The paper claimed the most likely explanation was an unusual weather event. The birds had no impact injuries evident from before the fall, no deadly disease. Their bodies just stopped working and down they went, to the abandoned baseball diamond right in the center of our small, recreational world.

Someone cleaned up the corpses right away, taking a significant number of the beer cans with them. I asked around to find out who it was, or what organization had the job of taking care of the dead birds, but came up empty. I'd loved birds since I was a girl, and whenever I felt alone in the world I would tell myself that one day I would grow up and find my proper flock. A tired metaphor, I know, but I was young and the phrase was new to me, felt as if it had been invented for me.

I went to the park when I knew no one would be there. I brought my guitar and sang a farewell song to the grass and felt comforted, though it had been meant to honor the birds. Perhaps I was really honoring the death of something in myself.

The following afternoon a huge winged creature appeared in the abandoned field. A few of the teenagers who'd been playing basketball in the adjacent new field said they heard a sound like an inverted *pop* and saw a cloud of purple smoke over the park. Others said they thought the noise they heard was a car backfiring, and didn't notice a cloud. Another group said they smelled something burning, and that a smoky haze hung in the air but there was no unusual sound.

I'd also been there, walking around for the sake of being outside. I experienced a moment of profound silence and a tickling sensation across my skin.

The creature was tall, imposing and quiet, with black wings that engulfed her like a fortress. A breeze ruffled her feathers to reveal a pale, angular face with skin so white it looked almost blue. As I glimpsed it, a name popped into my head, and I began to think of her as the Morrigan.

Storm clouds gathered in the sky and thunder sounded just before the police arrived. I thought of going home, but I didn't want to leave the Morrigan. I had no rational bond to her, other than my affection for birds.

Though the air was thick with moisture, there was no rain. I watched from a distance, heart pounding in my chest. I felt protective of her, afraid for her safety, but there was nothing that I could do.

They cast a commercial fishing net over her and began to pull the ends together. As the netting stretched tighter, she screeched and spread her wings. They dragged the net toward the Animal Control van. The net moved easily, but the creature did not go with it. Clouds parted for a moment and a ray of sunlight fell upon her wings, which glinted like metal. As the Animal Control people tugged at the net, it fell to shreds.

I looked back at the creature. Her head was tilted upwards, eyes closed, her face absorbing the last of that solitary ray of light. She had a long, curved beak and her eyes were set far apart on either side of her head but were oddly human. She lifted her feathers, and I caught a glimpse of their contours and got a sense of hard, razor-sharp edges.

I could not hear the authorities from where I stood, but several of their people got red in the face and made panicked gestures. I kept my distance. I had no ideas for them. I just wanted to be near the creature.

A beat-up pickup truck pulled up to the cops and the Animal Control van a few minutes later. It belonged to one of the local farmers. An older man and a teenaged boy got out, both wearing overalls and mud-covered boots. The boy went to the rear of the truck and stopped, staring at the Morrigan while his father—I assumed it was his father—went to talk to the authorities.

They conferred for a few minutes. The boy ignored them until the older man turned and called out to him. The boy nodded, and climbed in the truck's bed. He retrieved something long and metallic. It took me a moment to figure out what it was. A cattle prod. They were going to zap her with electricity to try to force her to move.

I swallowed, my mouth dry and my stomach queasy as I watched the boy hand it off to the old man, and the old man hand it off to one of the Animal Control men. A group of kids stood at the side of the road which separated the parking area from the old field, aiming their cell phones at the Morrigan, taking video.

A man from Animal Control crossed the field to get to the Morrigan. He called out, "Stay back!" and continued on his way. Those without cell phones listened and took a few steps back; the ones who were filming ignored the direction. I didn't want to watch, but couldn't look away as the man approached the Morrigan from behind and stretched out an arm to increase the reach of his cattle prod.

As soon as it contacted her back, he zapped her with it. Shimmering blue lines outlined every feather for a moment so brief I might have imagined it. There was a smell of burning flesh and smoke on the air. I recognized the smell—my husband had once taken a lighter to my arm. Reflexively I pulled the long sleeves of my sweater over my hands. The smell was the same, but stronger. The Animal Control man dropped to the ground. The Morrigan's feathers shook and then settled, beak tucked into her chest.

A teenager broke the silence first. "What the hell just happened?" The kid must have known that the charge in a cattle prod was not high enough to inflict the kind of damage we just witnessed.

A police officer rushed to the Animal Control person's side, knelt down and touched the man's neck. He looked out to the other officers and shook his head. I knew what that meant. Dead.

The prone body reminded me too much of my husband, gone a year. For a moment, the image of my husband lying on the kitchen floor next to a spilled liquor bottle superimposed itself over the dead man. I blinked the image away.

Another officer approached the group of teenagers. I didn't wait to hear what he had to say because I already knew what was next. Move along, nothing to see here, or something to that effect. I turned around and headed home. I didn't want to watch anyone else die, or see the Morrigan hurt by whatever they were going to try next.

It was hard not to look back toward her as I took the path back to my house. I felt like she was watching me.

I turned on the television and waited for the news to fill me in on what I missed. Shaky digital footage from one of the teenagers' cameras accompanied the anchor's recap, with a side note that the video had already gone viral on the web. The female field reporter mentioned a few other attempts to move the Morrigan. Deployed tranquilizer darts fell to the ground, useless, although when they were retrieved one of the personnel accidentally stabbed himself with it. He was now at the hospital, in stable condition, but under observation for the night.

The park was closed until the authorities could figure out the next step. Biologists were called in from local universities to consult. No further plans were released to the media. One professor stated that, "We're reluctant to do anything that might kill the creature. It's an undocumented species and to destroy it without learning more would be a great loss to science."

A spokesperson from the Centers for Disease Control expressed concern about potential diseases. "We don't know if this new animal is capable of spreading illness to other wildlife in the area or to humans. It could be carrying a new strain of bird flu. Any personnel who have to deal with the creature should, at the very least, protect themselves with latex gloves and a mask."

I thought of the authorities on the scene. None of them had taken such precautions.

Next, there were thoughts from PETA, then someone from a far-flung community who believed the story was a hoax. I thought they were milking the story, and turned it off when it became clear I wasn't going to learn any real information.

Weird dreams followed that night. Hazy melodies sang at the edge of consciousness. Wings sliced the air above me like blades but fell softly on my brow in a way that caressed. A feeling of vulnerability and love. Fear ending in violence. Vague impressions that made no sense. My husband's angry face, twisted in rage, floated by as if it were made of clouds.

The dream-feeling hung around after I woke up the next morning. Images of birds danced on the surface of my coffee and did not disperse until I drained the cup.

I felt pulled to go back to the park just to look at the Morrigan, but resisted by immersing myself in neglected tasks around the house. Standing on the throw rug which hid remnants of a dark stain left by my husband, I washed the dishes. I wiped coffee splatter off the countertops and swept. My movements were agitated. I hated that there were reminders of him, still.

I ran out of indoor chores and went outside to clean up the yard. Time to rake, clear out downed tree branches and random trash blown over from my neighbor's cans. Tasks that my husband used to do with a beer in hand to make it more pleasant.

The birds were gone when I went out to rake, a chore that I hate. I had to remind myself of its necessity, that my body needed the movement, that dead leaves are good in compost. It took all afternoon before I could sit and survey my work. I felt accomplished even as soreness began to steal over my muscles. I looked up at the trees and the crows were back. A lot of crows. A breeze kicked up, lifting loose feathers as the birds stared at me, mysterious and implacable.

It was only 5 p.m. but my bed seemed like the best place in the world to be. Heavy sleep and vivid dreams. Crunch of leaves. The humming sound as the Earth vibrated my feet. The Morrigan in the field with her face tilted up to the moon. Her wings spread wide open, as if getting ready for flight, razor's-edge feathers glinting silver. I stepped forward and she folded me in an embrace which was warm, too warm.

My eyes felt glued shut when I woke. The blankets were twisted and damp with sweat, sticking to my legs as I rolled over to look at the clock. It was 5 a.m.

The air should have been chilly so I got up to check the thermostat. I must have bumped it—the temperature was set to 70 degrees. Too high for the small space. My husband used to like the temperature high, but then he'd complain about the heating bill as if it was my fault. I frowned, then lowered it and put on a robe. Part of me wanted to go back to bed, but I had already slept too long. I made coffee and turned on the local morning news. The worried face of the field reporter was incongruous with the cheerful delivery of her words.

She was at the park, the field was cordoned off by police tape. The park entrances were barricaded with traffic cones and more tape. Police officers moved anonymously in the background of every shot. A local boy had gone missing. Last seen at the park by two friends who were, according to the reporter, in shock and unable to speak. The broadcast showed a jerky camera shot of the Morrigan with wings closed, head hidden. She stood on one claw.

A red baseball cap and one mangled sneaker with no sign of its partner lay a few feet away. These may have belonged to the missing teenager. Other items were recovered but these were close to the mystery creature. The reporter went on, "It is unclear to the authorities whether or not the presence of the creature has anything to do with the boy's disappearance, and they are urging anyone who might have seen something to come forward. It is also unclear how, or when, the boys were able to get past authorities into the park."

I swallowed hot coffee and burned my tongue.

My first thought was ungenerous. The boy probably got too close, did something to provoke her, everyone knows how teenaged boys can be. But then I thought of his family and friends, which made me ashamed for thinking that way. I didn't know anything about this kid, but anyone that young is still full of promise.

I was amazed that the Morrigan remained, that she hadn't been killed or taken away. It wasn't safe to go see her at the park. They needed to search the grounds for clues, evidence. There were safety concerns to the public, blah, blah, blah.

The rest of the day passed quietly, though I noticed more crows than usual gathering in the yard. I followed my normal routines, and fought urges to visit the Morrigan, and kept the television turned off.

The day after that, the park appeared on the news again. This time there were two missing teenaged girls. The broadcast showed video footage of empty desks and open lockers with personal items taped to the interior. Pictures of boyfriends. A shrine in the lobby with flowers and burning candles. The homage looked strange against institutional brick wall and tiled floor. The reporter mentioned grief counselors on hand to help students cope with the recent tragedies. A note was found, written by one of the girls. Ink dotted the page in splotches with black lettering, thick and harsh-looking. "She's calling me to judgment," was all it said.

The anchor said something about crowds gathering at the entrances to the park, urging them to listen to the authorities and disperse for public safety.

I shut off the television and inspected the cupboards in my kitchen. The contents were sparse and the need for food was a welcome distraction, but the news story followed me to the store. In the produce section I overheard two mothers talking to each other.

"I had the hardest time getting my girls to talk about it. I threatened to increase her visits to the child psychologist and finally she told me. I'm not sure I understand it, but at least I got her talking."

"At least you can afford to send your girl to talk to someone. Our church offers free services, but I'm not sure if it will do any good."

I grabbed a bag of sunflower seeds off the shelf so that I could listen without being too obvious.

"She said that the kids at school have been sneaking out to the park at night to look at that monster. Apparently it's the cool thing to do. But there are those missing kids. She said everyone knew he was going to see the creature but the kids are scared to say anything."

The other mom shook her head. "I don't like this. When are we going to get that thing out of our community?"

"I don't understand why it's still there. It hasn't moved. We don't know anything about it. If it dies out there it could be a huge health hazard. What if it's carrying diseases?"

As she spoke her voice increased in pitch and speed, signifying a buildup to frenzy. I wanted no part of that. Irrationally, I felt like I was under attack.

At night the call of the Morrigan came like a physical pressure. Around 3 a.m I couldn't take it anymore and ventured out. There were hidden paths between my house and the field. That's probably how those kids got through without being seen.

Leaves crunched under my feet creating a weird song with my breath and heartbeat. I thought I heard animals moving nearby and imagined large furry beasts with sharp teeth and big eyes, but I was more afraid of being found by another human. I was vulnerable, alone. Until that moment I never saw my habit of solitude as a problem. As I had that thought, I reached the old baseball field, and the Morrigan.

A police cruiser was parked across from the field. An officer was inside. As I passed, I saw his head tilted back. Light cast by a nearby lamp-post allowed me to see that his eyes were closed. I crept by, hoping he would remain asleep.

She was terrifying and lovely in the moonlight. Slowly her wings unfolded, and she opened toward me. Spotty patches of white down showed along her belly. Her head turned to the left and she stared at me with one eye. Her eyes were so large that even with only the light of the full moon I could see the pupils expand. She emitted a rumbling noise and I realized she was cooing.

I moved closer and her feathers puffed out slightly. The eye pointed my way slowly blinked. Closer.

The cooing sound got louder. Images and sensations that were new to me teased. My stomach drew tight as it fought the end-over-end feeling of moving swiftly through air at high altitudes. Though my feet were still connected to the ground, I saw misty mountain peaks, gray valleys, and cityscapes. Air so cold and then so warm kissed my skin. I felt pulled to land in order to eat, drink, and find a connection.

The Morrigan was alone. I understood why she came here. I could not stop from moving closer to her even as images of the missing students flooded my mind. She invited them into her embrace, looking for comfort, solace, a friend. Instead she found fear, anger, and danger lurking in the swift reflexes of young musculature. Rejection of the embrace. Instinct taking over. Unbearable sadness and a sense of loss even as she destroyed young lives with the sharp edges of her feathers.

In the distance I heard the police officer coming to life. The car door slamming shut, his footsteps on pavement, his voice calling out, "Hey, lady! Stop! You can't be here!" He was too far away and I too entranced.

Whether she would wound me, I did not know, but I accepted the embrace. She and I were the same. I have also sought love and ended up killing. I tried to forget, to pretend that my husband had left without an explanation. Which is, in a way, true.

How do you explain love turned sour, the fist raised one too many times, the heartbreak even as you deliberately sink the knife into someone's chest, knowing what it means?

Loss. An irrevocable end to further damage at the hands of another, yes, but also an end to the possibility of healing, redemption.

How does one explain that he disappeared deep under the garden where the tomatoes grow so big?

Yes, I accept the embrace, Morrigan. You can pierce me if you want to.

One-Hundred-Eye Curse

No one should be cursed with the ability to see so much.

One hundred eyes. One hundred opportunities for pink-eye infections. One hundred places for an untold number of eyelashes to get stuck. Dust is a nightmare. I cannot sleep.

This is too cruel a state for a giant to be in. Size alone makes solitude difficult. I cannot help but leave traces of myself with every step I take, though I cannot be properly stalked. Stealth will not help you. I see everything. I am Argus Panoptes.

I also know that a lot of people talk about me, that it is far from flattering and that I am totally misunderstood. I get it. I'm a giant, known for being grumpy and violent. It makes me glad that I only have two ears.

Most people can't see the gods unless the gods choose to be seen. I can see them. Most of the time, they hang out on Mount Olympus playing card games, eating, sleeping, having affairs. There are moments when the gods cannot help meddling with people. The results of alleviating their ennui are often catastrophic for the humans that have attracted their mercurial attentions. Later, these events become legend, celebrated stories that humans love, though they are fraught with blood and pain and loss. I do not understand the need to exalt such stories when there is enough blood and pain and loss in life without the gods—but then, I am not of mankind.

When Zeus gets bored, he always hunts for some new creature with which to experience carnal delights. My sympathies lie with his wife, Hera. She's just as bored with immortality as he is, but she doesn't go to bars or bathhouses trying to pick up young warriors. I have to admit, there might be a little bit of jealousy involved on my part. My size is fixed, unlike the gods who can shape-shift at will. There are not too many giantesses left in the world and most females of other species are either too deadly or too tiny for me to woo. It gets lonely.

So, of course when Hera asked me to keep all my eyes on her gorgeous white heifer, I agreed. I didn't have anything else to do except play golf with villagers. The villagers hated playing golf with me. They complained of injuries after I whacked them with my club; if I managed a long drive, they'd end up flailing around in the ocean for days.

Apparently, the villagers and I do not share the same sense of humor. For me, even the company of a cow was appealing. I should have known that the pledge of my services to a goddess would exact a price.

At first, I kept watch over the cow in the valley where Hera had found me. It was a muddy valley through which a river ran, but the water was filthy and the cow developed a cough. Her pristine white coat became caked with mud. Strange that the suffering of a cow should bother me when I have no empathy for the suffering of humans. Consider that the lives of domestic animals are shaped by human hands, human agendas, and human needs: their lives are never truly their own. Perhaps for this reason, I felt disposed to act more kindly.

I let the heifer think that I wasn't watching to see where she would go; I thought that her bovine instincts might lead us to better pastures. Cows are painfully slow. As she walked over the landscape, lowing constantly as if calling for someone, it occurred to me that a cow was poor company. There is nothing that a giant can do with a cow except eat it, and since I was bound by Hera to guard the stupid thing, I could not even do that.

Eventually, the cow came upon a well-kept farm, with ample fields for grazing and a clear stream running through it. It was a lucky find since much of the terrain on this island is rough and rocky, or plagued by carnivorous beasts. Eager for clean water to drink and bathe in, Hera's white cow ambled over to the stream. She lowered her head, and I observed that she must have caught sight of her reflection. She moved her head from side to side, as if surveying her own profile, as a human would. Her moo then had a quality of deep distress.

It puzzled me that a cow should be so concerned over her own appearance. I thought about Hera and then about Zeus, and scolded myself for not seeing it sooner. For a guy with a hundred eyes, sometimes my perception is a bit hazy. I suspected that this was no ordinary heifer. Knowing what I did about Zeus and Hera, I figured the cow to be a lovely maiden unwillingly transformed. Zeus was famous for his infidelities, as was Hera for her rage against any object of his affection. It raised a few questions. I wondered who the cow was and what she looked like in her natural form. Which member of the divine couple was responsible for the transforming Io into a cow? Did Zeus do it to protect the girl, or did Hera do it for spite? The detail was not very important to me personally, but it was something to occupy my thoughts and pass the time.

The cow calmed down. She plunged her head into the stream to drink, and once she had her fill, she crossed the stream and walked toward the house.

It wasn't long before she encountered a few humans. A couple of little girls and a man approached. The girls stroked her chest and forelegs, and the man scratched behind her ears. I watched from behind a cluster of tall trees as the cow scratched her name in the sand on the bank of the stream. The little girls started crying and the man wept openly. I tried to turn my eyes away out of politeness, but getting all one hundred of them diverted at once is impossible. It only confirmed my suspicion that the cow was human. These people were her family.

Normally I am not a compassionate giant, but watching the father weep and throw his arms around his daughter's unnaturally wide neck softened me toward the cow. I understood that in her transformed state it would be as painful to stay with her kin as to leave them behind. Like me, she was doomed to be misunderstood. Sure, as a cow she was pretty limited, but Io and I had something in common. We were both freaks, isolated. In contemplative moments, I wondered which of us suffered more. Was it worse to have known love and fellowship and lost those precious commodities, or to have never experienced those things and long to know about them? My mind could never settle the question.

Dusk fell and her family went inside. The goodbyes were tearful, but they did not ask if she would stay. I like to think that they knew she could not.

Once out of hiding, I guided Io to a valley I knew of where there were no humans, where another stream ran clean and clear and the grass grew lush. A gently sloped mountain covered in tall, wild grasses in shades of yellow and green overlooked the valley. Near the crest there was a rocky outcrop with an unobstructed view to Io's pasture. The sturdy flat plane of its surface was perfect for stretching my weary back in repose and I would be able to see any predators coming toward her, and—more germane to Hera's purposes—visitors or thieves.

Io and I lived there peacefully for a while. The days and nights were long. I had thought that the presence of another lonely soul, no matter how uncommunicative, would be of some comfort to me, but watching over Io had the opposite effect. I felt more trapped by existence than ever, and her mournful lows seemed to express the same sadness I felt. I am ashamed to say that I wept. Since my tears spilled from all one hundred eyes, I sometimes told myself that it was only the rain.

One late afternoon I found myself in a more contented mood than usual. Io's lowing had given way to pleasant, thoughtful silence which released me from the yoke of pondering forced solitude. I was cleaning out my ears with the leafy end of a tree branch when I heard the most beautiful music coming from a copse of pine.

All one hundred of my eyes blinked simultaneously in drowsiness. That had never happened to me before, and the sensation was thrilling. It made the notion of total rest seem possible. The idea of dreams seduced me into inviting the musician to come closer and sit next to me on a bench made from an olive tree I had felled.

The man stepped out of the woods and I recognized him immediately. Hermes is hard to misidentify. There is no one else in all the pantheon tacky enough to wear winged sandals and a half-bowl helmet with wings. He always claimed it had to do with aerodynamics, but personally, I think he likes to stand out in a crowd.

I offered him some berry wine and some fresh-cooked deer meat, which he accepted cheerfully. I invited him to play more of his music and asked about the instrument, a flute made of several reeds of varying lengths lashed together.

I told Hermes that the music allowed all my eyes to close at once, and how it gave me such great relief. He asked if I wanted to try and sleep, adding, "It must be difficult to have so many eyes. It would give me pleasure to give you some temporary ease."

He took up his flute and began to play a soft, slow melody. I nodded my head and then, after a few measures, I fell asleep. All one hundred eyes closed. It felt glorious to enter that state of temporary oblivion that every man and beast has enjoyed since the dawn of time! I rested, truly, allowing the music to filter into dreams, where it mingled with Io's lows and the voice of a giantess conjured by my imagination.

Soon, my one giantess turned into one hundred, a woman of my own size to please each eye. They danced and blew kisses at me from the edge of a field filled with cows sizeable enough to provide a full meal, rather than the teasing, savory snack they were in my waking life. Old defeated enemies bowed before me—the serpent-legged Echidna, the rabid bull of Arcadia. These creatures thanked me for granting them honorable deaths. The giantesses sang my praises and offered gifts. I was given a keg of wine to quench my thirst and a large pillow on which to lay my head. These were the comforts of smaller men, comforts my size had always precluded.

The dancers were just beginning to relieve themselves of clothing when the dream abruptly stopped. My inner world went dark, and when I attempted to open my eyes, I found that I could not.

I mourned the loss of my dream, not knowing what had happened. I heard the voices of Hera and Zeus.

Hera shouted, "You had Hermes kill him to free that stupid heifer!"

"So what if I did?" Zeus thundered. "It was not Io who did you wrong!"

The two squabbled longer, but I was too busy berating myself for trusting the gods. It was unfair to lose the bliss of dreams at the moment of their discovery. Seething with the sense of betrayal, I roared but to no effect. I was dead.

Not even vanquished Sirens can break the sound barrier between the afterlife and the land of the living. My lingering consciousness could do nothing but act as witness.

Zeus and Hera stood over my corpse, on opposite sides, facing each other. Hera's veil fluttered with the force of her words as she shouted at Zeus. The pomegranate she carried squirted juice down the front of her matronly dress, giving the impression of fresh-spilled blood; the only evidence of Zeus's inner turmoil showed in the flickering of the lightning bolt he carried in his left hand. They shouted threatened and pleaded with each other until each wept tears of regret. Lacking a body with which to smash and squash and kill, I had hoped for a different ending to this feud. Disappointed that they did not kill each other, I could not, for some reason, turn away.

Only after a pitiful reconciliation did they come to an agreement regarding Io. Zeus promised never to stray from the marriage bed again, and Hera promised to let Io go, and return her to human form. But both Zeus and Hera were treacherous, and I vaguely recall thinking that Zeus lied and Hera was sure to twist her promise. Though I had concerns for Io, I was more concerned for myself. Where would I go now that I was dead?

I stared at my body. The huge, one-hundred-eyed head had been severed from the body at the neck. Never had I so desired to cry. I wanted my eyes back so that my tears might flow as freely as those of the distraught gods.

Zeus departed, leaving Hera to tend to the body. The goddess whistled, and a bevy of peacocks waddled clumsily across the rocky outcrop. Their squawks sounded like screaming women, similar to Hera's shrill voice when she fought with Zeus. I had heard they were her favorite among the birds.

She spoke to my corpse, not knowing that my consciousness hovered.

"I will burn your body, noble Argus, but to honor you I shall have your eyes set forever in the feathers of my peacocks, that you may always be remembered."

That was some comfort. Though still annoyed that I had become a casualty of the war between Hera and Zeus, I felt pleasure at being deemed noble.

Hera harvested all one hundred eyes and wove them into the peacocks' feathers as she promised. Though I had no ears, I heard the wet squish of my dead eyes as Hera's fingers punctured them with peacock quills. If a soul could wince, mine would have. She poked and wove, each stitch a bit of tiny, meticulous violence more deliberate and disturbing than any slaughter I had been responsible for in life. The peacocks proved unfeeling birds, but perhaps they did not know that the ornaments Hera wove into their colorful feathers once belonged to a living creature. The spread their feathers and shook them, pranced back and forth in front of each other showing off the emblems of my death as if they were jewels. The only mercy contained in the act was that I could not feel the harsh manipulation of each exposed eye.

It was all wrong. In death, we are meant to have either the heavens or Tartarus; but when she grafted my eyes onto those gaudy feathers, she bound my consciousness to Earth. Though I am dead, and Io long gone, I remain Argus Panoptes, cursed to be in death as I was in life. I see everything, and for me there is no rest.

Famous Nudes in Winter Clothing

Raeburn Stewart, director of the Davidson Art Gallery, had reservations about the much-publicized opening of Edmund Joel's show. Edmund's unpredictability was legend, and so true a quality of this rising star that even when critics and gossip columnists speculated that an innocuous title could actually be some terrifying but undeniably innovative visual commentary on something controversial, the exhibition might just contain paintings and sculptures of puppies. The board expected *Famous Nudes in Winter Clothing* to be a simple but thought-provoking artistic novelty. It seemed hardly controversial to paint winter clothing on formerly nude figures from famous paintings, except for the inevitable grumbles brought on by altering classic paintings by long-dead artists. They anticipated a lively debate about post-modernism, post-post-modernism and perhaps even collage art, but Stewart's instincts told him to expect something less comfortable from Edmund Joel. Stewart had no personal qualms about controversy in art, but he preferred to keep controversy away from his gallery.

The artist delivered the paintings to the gallery as they were completed, one at a time. Stewart asked Edmund why he was handling the delivery in a way that created extra work.

"I just feel like it," Edmund said.

Edmund needed the space. His ex-fiancé, punk singer Wina Alpha, had recently ended their engagement by having the locks changed at his apartment. She had waited on the third floor balcony for him to pass by and then tossed down a regulation life-saver on which she wrote, in florescent pink nail polish, "U R ded 2 me. Wur ovah."

Wina waited for Edmund to get the message and then dragged her new lover onto the balcony for a kiss that looked savage and unsexy to Edmund. He instantly fell out of love with Wina, and waved goodbye.

Now he missed the apartment, which covered the whole floor of the building; all of that art space gone with one illicit kiss. Edmund felt more upset about the apartment than about Wina. *I guess I don't know my own heart.*

The result of Edmund's personal drama was that *Famous Nudes in Winter Clothing* had to be painted in a small, boxy studio apartment with a spacious fire escape landing. It was temporary, just until his business managers were able to sort out the problem of his old lease. The upside was that the limited space prevented him from accumulating too much stuff; the downside was that he could only store one painting at a time. It was characteristic of Edmund to feel aesthetically offended by his own creations as soon as they were finished. With no space and not enough linen, he had nowhere to place them out of his line of sight. It never occurred to him that he could simply flip the paintings to face the wall.

Famous Nudes in Winter Clothing was a particularly unsettling series. After having applied common winter outerwear to the figures of Botticelli, Michelangelo and Da Vinci, among others, Edmund could not help the nagging sensation that the work had *marketing* potential. Not that he had a problem with marketing, but this was not the kind of artist he wanted to be. He could already envision his concept being used in fashion magazines. If it had not been for Wina Alpha's cruel hijacking of his apartment, he would have aborted the project, and damn the gallery's pursuit of damages in civil court for breaking his contract.

Edmund hatched a plan to emphasize the point of the series, to ensure he provoked the discussion he intended and avoid having his idea co-opted to sell winter sportswear. He placed an anonymous ad in the local paper looking for nude art models, male and female, aged twenty-one to seventy. He didn't hide this activity from the gallery, but neither did he mention it.

Raeburn Stewart should have been reassured by the paintings as they arrived. The first one was a revision of Albrecht Dürer's *Adam and Eve*. Adam wore a long leather trench coat and heavy boots, while Eve was decked out in a cumbersome pink snow suit, ear muffs and mittens. The fig leaves remained in place over their respective genitalia, which made Stewart smile. He wasn't sure how he felt about the awkward way that the apple rested in Eve's be-mittened hand, or the slightly surprised expression on the serpent, but those were details for the critics to quibble about.

Boticelli's *Birth of Venus* also possessed a few touches of humor. Edmund had removed the secondary figures of the original painting, perhaps to highlight the warmth of the environment keep the focus on the central figure of Venus, emerging from a calm and happy sea in a clam shell. She was burdened by a plaid wool pea coat and leg warmers, though her feet remained bare. Sweat glistened on her otherwise unblemished forehead.

Hieronymus Bosch's vision of Hell from *The Garden of Earthly Delights* appeared more uncomfortable with Edmund's additions of blizzard-proof jackets, long johns, crocheted scarves and fur-lined hats with ear flaps. As paintings began to accrete, Stewart thought that each famous scene grew more profane with modern clothing on the previously nude figures.

He wondered if his familiarity with the original works of art colored his perception. Each of the original pieces being mimicked represented a gold standard of painterly skill as perceived during their time in history. But perhaps the discomfort had a simpler source: what if, in spite of all the academic language and analysis and supposed allegorical meaning attributed to fine art, the pleasure that he derived could be reduced to the idea that he liked looking at naked people? He had to admit that Edmund was onto something; perhaps this was a conversation worth having.

While Stewart pondered the significance and implications of Edmund's art, Edmund met his potential models at the Round Hole Donut Shop. The artist identified himself by a paper rose pinned to the lapel of his green polyester sport coat. The potential models identified themselves to him by asking, "You the guy looking for models?"

Most responding to the ad were white men over forty who were down on their luck. Edmund had been hoping for a more diverse group, but he had only a day to the opening of *Famous Nudes in Winter Clothing*. There was no time to combat homogeneity.

Only four women showed up; a fifty-something African-American woman named Nan with amazing, long, beaded braids, and an Asian woman with cheerful eyes, a thick accent and a heavily lined face that he found intriguing. The other two were girls in their twenties who wore heavy make-up and tight black dresses with pink ballet sweaters and contradictory ratty old sneakers. He bought everyone coffee, offered a couple of the men the use of his shower after the meeting, and explained exactly what he wanted.

After the explanation, most of the men and the Asian woman left, thanking him for the coffee. "I'm just not that brave," explained one of the men.

The Asian woman wagged a finger at Edmund and said, "You paint, I pose. That all." One of the younger girls also had to bow out. "I'm working tomorrow night. Can't do it." He thought Nan would also bow out, and looked at her expectantly. She caught the look and laughed. "Spent half my life at Rainbow gatherings and such. You don't have to worry about me."

Edmund, alarmed that he only had seven models willing to carry out his plan, turned to the other young girl. "What about you? Can you commit?"

She shrugged, "Yeah. Anything is better than the work I'm doing now."

Edmund didn't ask for fear of chasing her away.

The day of the opening arrived, but only five of the models did. Nan and the girl—whose name was Pam—and three men: Mike, Joe, and Bob.

Raeburn Stewart let them in to the locked gallery an hour before the exhibit was to begin. Edmund's entourage provided him with a rising sense of foreboding. They all wore white terry cloth robes, shoes, and nothing else.

"I knew it," he muttered.

The group filed past him through the glass door. Edmund was the first inside the gallery. He checked that his paintings were hung properly and the lighting was satisfactory. Stewart's assistant, Kay, was preoccupied with setting out canapés, along with bottles of wine and glasses, on a table along the rear wall, her back to the room.

After the last of Edmund's models filed in, Stewart locked the door behind them and hurried to Edmund's side. One of the men reached his assistant and said, "Hey, no one said there would be free booze. Cool!"

She jumped a little and squealed as he reached for the glass of red she had just poured.

"Edmund, what is this?" Stewart asked.

Edmund's sideways glance felt dismissive. "Oh. Just the final part of the exhibit."

"Okay. But what exactly are these people doing here?"

One of the men approached, his robe draped over his arm. "So, what do we do with these?"

"Oh, dear Lord," Stewart said when confronted with the naked stranger. "Edmund, you can't be serious."

Edmund ignored Stewart as he addressed the model. "Keep that on until my friend here has a chance to cover the windows. Then there's a room in the back that I'll show you."

"Okay." The model put his robe back on, but left it hanging open. The belt hung from only one loop and dragged across the cream-colored tiled floor.

Edmund looked at Stewart, hands tensed at his sides as if preparing for a fight. "It's art. Nudes are in the title, Raeburn. So, put your disclaimer on the door and paper the windows. You've done this before." Edmund slapped him on the back and gave him a wink. "You think I haven't read up on you and the place?"

Stewart said, "That was fifteen years ago. Things are different, now."

Edmund was already walking away, toward the models.

Stewart watched as the group gathered in a circle around the artist. He hated to admit that Edmund had a point. The gallery had papered the windows for controversial exhibits in the past. That didn't mean it was a good experience, and there had been no live nudes in the room. Another difference that Stewart thought particularly significant was the fact that the gallery, and therefore the local press, had fair warning for the previous event. Tonight's audience would not be prepared.

Judging by the tortured expression of Kay's face as she hurried toward him, she shared his concern. Stewart was comforted that there was at least one other person in the room who was on his side.

Kay said, "Rae? What do we do? I'm not sure if we have enough wine. These people -"

So it isn't the nudity that bothers her, he thought. *Maybe I'm too uptight.*

"I need you to line the windows with paper as quickly as you can. Don't worry about the wine. We still have that case of cheap stuff for emergencies if we need it. And put the disclaimer on the door," he barked as he took his cell phone out of his pocket. "I have a lot of phone calls to make in a very short amount of time."

He hurried toward the back of the gallery, leaving the bright space for the darker, cozier environs of his office. He kept a bottle of scotch in his desk. This was an occasion that called for it.

He called each member of the board and explained the situation. Reactions were mixed. Some of them laughed and said it was good publicity. One of them asked if the models were attractive. Another didn't seem to care about potential controversy or the subject of the art as long as he got to have his photo taken with the artist. Others were alarmed and threatened Stewart's job. He could only hope that the board members with the opposite perspective would prevail in that discussion. Things were in motion. If he did lose his job, he could always part with some art and retire on the sales, though Stewart loathed the idea.

The next batch of calls were to media outlets who had been expecting to cover the exhibit from inside the gallery.

It was part of his job to alert them to the changed situation. No photography, no video. There had been no warning about the models and therefore no time for the gallery to prepare release forms. Stewart, not being privy to the exact details of the contract they'd made with Edmund, would be the party responsible if one of them got upset about a picture in the paper or a digitally blurred video on television. It annoyed him that he had to think in these terms. Logically, one might assume that a person willing to appear in the nude in a relatively public space was unlikely to get upset about a photo, but then people were not always logical. Art was not always logical.

Stewart emerged from his office just in time for the gallery's front door to open. Kay had called in extra security personnel to check identification. He was grateful that she had thought of that. It was difficult to ignore the naked bodies of Edmund's models, and he worried that the Davidson's gallery patrons would spend more time staring at them than at the art.

Edmund sat on a cream-colored bench in the center of the gallery with a bottle of red wine. There were no dark corners to hide in if anything went wrong, no easy escape route. Once the exhibit began, the door leading to offices and storage space would be locked. He fought his nervousness by eavesdropping on the models.

Nan stood with two of the men—Mike and Joe, if Edmund recalled correctly—in front of the winterized *Death and the Maiden*.

Joe said, "I thought these were supposed to be naked people?"

Nan laughed and answered, "Honey, *we* are the naked people. Best get comfortable with that."

Across the room, Pam stood alone. She held a glass of wine as casually as if she were clothed. Her head was tilted slightly to the side, the pose of a person in serious contemplation of art. Edmund picked up his open bottle of wine and approached from behind.

"What do you think?" he asked.

Pam did not turn to look at him. "I'm not sure yet. Is it supposed to be funny?"

The painting in front of them was a redux of one of Cezanne's many bathers. Edmund had given her an oversized, purple down-stuffed winter coat, possibly the tackiest of the coats in all the paintings, but she still held a washcloth over her pudenda.

"There are intentional elements of humor, yes, but that isn't the point."

"Hmm," said Pam. Her tone was non-committal and Edmund did not know her well enough to know if it meant that she was thinking about the art or if she was disinterested. He was pretty sure he liked that about her.

"So are you going to take your clothes off, too?" she asked.

Edmund looked at her, surprised. She kept her gaze on the painting, but began walking away so that he was forced to follow her to the next one. "I hadn't thought of it."

Pam took a sip from her glass. "You should."

Edmund laughed. "Are you saying you want to see me naked?"

Little vertical creases appeared in Pam's forehead, and Edmund blushed, knowing that he had annoyed her with his lame attempt at flirting.

"No." Pam turned and looked Edmund in the face, a half-smile playing on her lips. "I'm saying have some balls.

Participate in your own idea and be less of a voyeur. You think it's an easy thing to be this vulnerable in a public space? To be aware of yourself as an object?"

Edmund swallowed and looked away from Pam. "I never thought about it."

She touched his elbow. "Look, I don't know you. I'm not saying you're a jerk, or anything. But don't you think, as an artist, it might be interesting to be part of the art in a way that's maybe new to you? Find out what this feels like?"

Edmund looked into Pam's eyes. "You have a point."

She smiled. "I know."

She walked away from him, toward Nan, Mike, and Joe. Edmund stared after her, but made no move to join his models. He took a swig from his bottle of wine and muttered, "Fuck."

The last time he'd been nude in a public space was in college, skinny-dipping, drunk, under the cover of darkness. Light would expose all his flaws, not to mention the last punk rock experiment he shared with Wina. She had marked him. To be nude meant putting that mark on display, to be reminded of that relationship when he wanted to forget. Even though he was afraid, he knew he was going to accept Pam's challenge. For art, anything. Perhaps the act could heal him in some way.

Stewart hoped the clamminess of his hands was not noticeable as he greeted the gallery's guests and urged them to sign the guest book. The turnout was higher than expected and he had no hope of remembering names. He wondered if the high attendance was due to Edmund's reputation or the presence of the nude models. Word-of-mouth about such things had a way of spreading fast.

Once the arrivals began to slow down, it was his job to mingle, discuss the art and hopefully then sell some of it. He hadn't been in a room with naked strangers since college art class. The clothed patrons kept a certain amount of distance from Edmund's models and spoke in whispers. Out of the corner of his eye, Stewart saw people pointing at body parts. He heard giggles, and cringed inwardly. At least the serious art people kept their expressions stoic and non-committal. There wasn't much chatter from them, more silent contemplation and chin-stroking, which in Stewart's experience could be very good for the gallery. It meant lengthy articles about the event in all the right places, no matter the verdict on the art.

An hour into the exhibit, the whispers, giggles and pointing had subsided, and Stewart allowed himself to relax, until he noticed Edmund sitting on the bench, rolling an empty bottle of red between his hands. Watching the artist made him feel nauseous. He could feel the pores on his face squeezing out beads of perspiration.

He wiped his brow with a monogrammed handkerchief and walked over to Edmund. Stewart picked up the bottle. "You drank this whole thing in an hour?"

Edmund nodded. "Need some liquid courage to get through this thing."

"Let me take that," Stewart said. He grabbed the bottle, worried that drops of red might spill and leave difficult stains on the cream colored tile. He walked through the gallery and unlocked the back door to get to his office. The door closed, Stewart allowed himself a growl of frustration, punched his oak desk (which bruised his knuckles), and took a swig from his bottle of scotch. Not enough to get drunk, just enough to get rid of the sharp edges. He hadn't signed up to baby-sit a drunk Edmund. Anxiety made him feel numb.

Stewart slowly straightened his tie, smoothed his hair, readjusted his glasses, and put the bottle of scotch back in his desk. Leaving the office to brave the rest of the event, his heart sank when he saw Kay running toward him.

"Edmund is taking his clothes off. I tried to get him to stop, but—"

Stewart groaned, "Oh, God."

"He's standing on top of the bench, leaving shoe prints all over it," Kay added.

"Shit."

Stewart hurried out to the gallery. Kay rushed along behind him. She was so close on his heels that she stepped on the back of his shoes, making for a clumsy re-entrance. No one saw them stumbling over each other.

The gallery's patrons were completely silent, staring at Edmund on top of the bench. He had posed himself like David. The artist's eyes were glassy, blank as the eyes of the original marble statue. He still had his shoes on and his pants puddled around his ankles.

Some of the patrons backed away from the spot as they continued to stare at Edmund. Stewart followed the direction of their collective gaze to Edmund's patch of pubic hair, which had a stripe in the middle that was dyed bright purple, a hue that Stewart would later learn matched his own face as he clutched his chest and fell to the floor.

Aliens in the Soda Machine

"Welcome to All Angles, your radio connection to those places where angels fear to tread and which scientists ignore. Or perhaps I should say that we go to those places where angels exist and where humanity has shuttered the windows of its collective soul—which is to say that perhaps the only reason we don't experience the presence of angelic beings is that we have closed our eyes to them.

I'm Norman Jacobs, and tonight our guest is an expert on Angelology. She is a writer of fiction, mythology and the New Age. Like Cher, she goes by only one name, Alana; and unlike Cher, she keeps her identity a secret. We'll talk to her about why; and you, dear listeners, will get a chance to talk to her as well a little later tonight, when we come back to explore the existence of angels on All Angles."

Norman forwarded through the long commercial set. The jingles and catch phrases played often enough in the studio and on the air five nights a week that he heard them play back in his head in spite of the fact that he was able to skip them during weekly performance checks. A twenty-year veteran and veritable rock star of the talk show radio format, Norman enjoyed an unprecedented sense of job security in the radio industry. He and his show, All Angles, had not only weathered the storm of the digital revolution, but flourished. Broadcasting on the internet earned the show new followers and only increased his international cult status as a connoisseur of the weird. He was a legend, and there was no need for him to endure evaluations of his own performance as a talk show radio announcer to check for verbal redundancies or mispronunciations. All regionalisms had been beaten out of him. His vigilance was unnecessary, but Norman was a man of habit, and in the back of his mind was a persistent fear that he would wake up one day and find his high level of eloquence demolished by unforeseen circumstances. This type of performance check was normally performed by a program director, but there was no one else around with Norman's long history of on-air experience. The only person qualified to evaluate him was himself.

This process was not all drudgery for Norman. He could not help feeling a little thrill when a guest was prompted into an epiphany by his own insightful questions, or led toward a new line of inquiry as a result of their discussions. Norman flushed with pleasure at the sound of his own voice delivering a particularly well-turned phrase. These little moments of joy were always more intense when these vocal pearls were dropped in a spirit of spontaneity: it made Norman sometimes feel that the universe spoke through him. Other times, listening to himself, his heart sank, and he felt that the universe didn't give a crap about him or his show, and that his twenty—year investment of time and emotion in the show had no point at all, and he might better serve humanity and the universe by becoming a farmer.

He only expressed such doubts to his cat, who was indifferent to his existential angst but managed to reassure him just by being there. If, as his guest Alana suggested, angels were truly everywhere, Norman was convinced that his cat, Art, was one of them. Art never failed to lift Norman's black moods. Of course, whenever a new story about the paranormal, or lost esoteric knowledge, came to his attention, Norman felt refocused and rejuvenated. He loved such subjects and felt that the well of what could be known, guessed, and speculated about was infinitely deep.

Fans and listeners could be amazing, brilliant people, or hostile and damaged; sometimes one caller could be both at the same time. He loved that these people wanted to connect with him and his guests, but he feared it, too. There were interns in place to screen callers, but inevitably a few slipped through; the sweet granny who said that she loved the show but worried that experts on aliens in the bible might go to hell; the self-proclaimed messiahs or antichrists; people who at first seemed coherent and then started to tell off-topic stories that had no beginning, middle, or end. Norman knew this was part of the landscape, and found comfort in the fact that he could always disconnect the call.

As many strange or unhinged callers as All Angles attracted, there was only one who consistently disturbed him—the woman with the sultry voice.

The woman with the sultry voice would call in on the hotline, always from a different number so that caller-id was useless in identifying her before she took up coveted on-air time. Her mantra, each time, was the same.

"Norman Jacobs, you are my soul mate. I am an alien/human hybrid and I will show you the wonders of the universe if you let me. If you do not let me—"

Norman or an intern always disconnected the call in the same spot. For the first year, the call came sporadically. Sometimes two nights in a row and then nothing for a few months, then every night for a week.

At first, it was funny, particularly to guest announcers and audio engineers. "She sounds hot, Norman. What's she doing chasing after you?" joked guest host Chuck Mars.

After a year of these calls, it stopped being funny. The studio installed security cameras in the hallways and all the entrances, and Norman installed his own security system at his house. He started carrying a rape whistle.

A self-proclaimed investigator of the paranormal, he had attracted his fair share of strange sensations and unexplained phenomena. Norman had seen UFOs and ghostly orbs, though he never had an alien encounter as far as he knew. He has heard disembodied voices and experienced past-life hypnosis. He had psychics tell him about himself in such detail that it made him want to weep. He had phone calls from listeners on the run from government agents, and phone calls from those who claimed to *be* government agents in charge of liquidating people. None of these things had brought Norman Jacobs to his knees. These experiences filled him with awe and curiosity, but never fear. The woman caller produced the fear that the paranormal could not.

Norman restarted the recording of the previous night's show just as the out queue for Bunker Foods signaled the end of a commercial. His own voice announced, "We're back on All Angles talking about the existence of angels..."

He winced. After every break he announced, "We're back," and it always made him cringe. This simple, repetitive phrase was something that radio announcers called "a crutch." Crutches were far more permissible in talk radio format, but Norman felt he leaned on this one too heavily. Still, he was hard pressed to imagine a better segue into a segment of talk.

Norman sighed and sat back in his chair, listening to himself for just a few minutes longer. It was becoming more difficult to sit through recent taped broadcasts of some shows. He'd visited the subject of angels many times on his show in the past and found himself apathetic toward the act of listening to the show now.

On the production desk in front of him was a hand-made card from his admirer. No stamp, no return address.

The card possessed a sort of primacy as an object in the room. It could not simply be set aside to be examined until Norman was done with his spot check; it demanded attention. The ominous piece of mail caused Norman to shut off the tape of angels before he completed his task.

The card, constructed of red poster-board, had been cut imprecisely, so that the edges of the card did not quite meet. Norman imagine that the slightly off slant of the card's pages said something—probably quite a lot—about the woman who sent it. The front was covered in messy glitter and paste that appeared to have originally been intended to be in the shape of a heart, but had been smeared so that glitter strayed from the heart outline and mixed in creepy, organic-looking blobs in random areas. It looked like a small child's craft work shoved into an envelope before it had dried. Beneath the glittery smears was writing in magic marker. She had printed the words, "Two Hearts Beat as One," the title of a U2 song that Norman often used to buffer segments of the show.

The interior of the card was a sloppy collage. His stalker had used so much glue that it bled through the glossy paper. The images were obviously taken from different magazines, although Normal could not discern which ones. Some of the images did not make immediate sense. A bird in the upper left corner. Several disembodied hands clearly ripped from ads for jewelry. One large blue eye in the right-hand corner. An image of the pyramid from the US one-dollar bill, possibly meant to allude to the Illuminati conspiracy.

Norman could not be sure of the specific intent behind the card without talking to his stalker, which was not anything he was interested in doing.

In the middle of this messy collection of images was the abdomen and torso of a pregnant woman. The head had been removed in favor of a stick figure's head with stars for eyes. The stars appeared to have been made with the application of Wite-Out around the head in block letters were written the words, "We will make Star Seed."

Red paint had been flung, Jackson Pollock style, across the entire thing. Was this just an artistic flourish, or was it meant to represent the blood it so resembled? The reference to star seed had to do with a theory among ufologists that human beings contain DNA from extraterrestrial beings, with some individuals' alien DNA more prevalent than others. Apparently, Norman Jacobs' stalker had decided that they were to make a baby together that more closely resembled some off-world species than a human being.

Norman no longer felt like being in the studio. Unlike many of the other station employees, he cleaned up after himself. He tossed his empty cup of coffee and his fast food wrapper into an overflowing garbage can and wiped the desk, which bore crumbs that were mostly not his. He was tempted to leave the star seed card there. He didn't want to acknowledge the thing, much less take it home. He wanted the object far away from him; but if the stalker's behavior escalated and put him in real danger, the card might be useful for the cops. If he left it at the studio it was likely to get lost.

Norman also had a slight knowledge of forensics from his guests on the show and, of course, television. If he left the card at the studio, any sort of DNA or fingerprint evidence it bore might disappear through contamination. He needed to find an envelope or a plastic bag, which meant that before he left he would have to rummage through the lounge.

The lounge looked like it belonged in a college dormitory. There was a circular orange Formica table in the center of the room, accompanied by plastic chairs and a couple of metal stools. A dusty lava lamp stood atop a bookshelf in the southwest corner. The bookshelf held piles of radio trade magazines, a huge dictionary, and a random catalogue of assault rifles. No one knew where the catalogue had come from, but the cover was creased and covered in greasy fingerprints and it was dated February 1992. Because of its age and mysterious origins, no one bothered to remove it. Much like the lava lamp, it was a piece of kitsch that added a certain amount of character to the space, although what *sort* of character was up for debate.

The floor was tiled with a gray and white faux marble linoleum covered in spots by mismatched throw rugs. A pale green couch stood along the left-hand wall. It was hard and uncomfortable. Norman never sat there, but he'd noticed that all new employees and interns tried it at least once.

Next to the couch was an old entertainment console that was used as the resting spot and operations area for the coffee maker. Someone kept a box of large freezer bags in the drawer that had once been designated as a place for VHS tapes. This was indicated by the presence of a plastic insert screwed to the interior of the drawer. He loved the way obsolete technology left its mark on furniture long after it was gone. Younger generations puzzled over the purpose of some of these things, which made Norman feel like he knew a secret.

He opened the drawer and pulled out a freezer bag, unzipped the seal, and placed the star seed stalker's card inside, then resealed it and placed the whole bag inside a book written by a prominent physicist he was hoping to interview on the show. He hoped that by the time the producers of All Angles got her on his program, the problem of the star seed stalker would be resolved.

Norman turned away from the coffee machine to face the soda machine on the opposite wall, and frowned. It wasn't good that in the past twenty minutes the stalker had procured a catchy moniker, even if it was only evident, so far, in his thoughts. He would not be able to resist saying it out loud in the presence of someone else, and once *that* happened it would catch like a spark on dry wood.

Norman stared at the soda machine, another piece of equipment from a bygone era. The machine's glowing face showed a fading panorama of giant water drops, with subtle shading. Some of the smaller blue and white droplets had been shaded in such a way that if you stared at the machine long enough, faces emerged inside the droplets—faces that looked like popular descriptions of aliens.

The machine itself had taken a bit of a beating over time. Labels under the buttons had degraded and been replaced by index cards with sloppy handwriting to indicate the type of soda which matched each button. A series of irregular scratches peppered the surface, but the weird aliens inside the machine persisted. One of the sound engineers had circled an alien water droplet in the bottom right corner using a red permanent marker. A thought bubble hovering over the alien's head said, "Hi Norman!" The red had long since faded to pink. It tickled Norman to overhear interns or new employees ask, "Why is that there?" only to realize months later that there were aliens in the soda machine, aliens whose faces looked strangely like shaded water droplets. The inside joke had gone on for at least a decade, but Norman never tired of it—he found its persistence reassuring. All he had to do was catch a glimpse of the aliens in the soda machine and he felt like all was right with his corner of the world.

As a result, on this particular evening, he was in a good mood when he left the building and entered the parking lot.

The sky was an ominous mix of purple and orange as dusk fell. Tonight, Norman had a rare night off. Guest hosts handled All Angles on Saturday and Sunday nights, which gave Norman an opportunity to catch up on his reading and do a little sky-watching from his yard. Sometimes on weekends he traveled, appearing at conferences or as a guest on other types of broadcasts concerning the paranormal, but this weekend was for rest.

Several cars were in the lot, but there were no people and very little traffic on the adjacent country road. There was no wind, which meant the autumn leaves that normally made all kinds of sound were silent as Norman moved from the building and across the asphalt to his car door. A smell like rotten eggs hung in the air. He tried to hold his breath but that only intensified the smell.

Norman glanced over his shoulder, thinking that perhaps the star seed stalker had left some sort of unpleasant surprise in the parking lot. In his peripheral vision he saw flashing lights, and turned in that direction.

A blurry gray disc hovered above the distant tree line, the lights seeming to come from the bottom of the disc and firing off at regular intervals in a circular pattern, like an LED display. The smell and eerie silence no longer mattered.

Norman stared at the disc for a few minutes before it occurred to him that he could use his cell phone to take a photo of the UFO. Anticipation and fear caused him to fumble in his pocket; his fingers kept sliding past the smooth surface of his cell phone, but he finally got a firm grip on it and turned it on. He aimed the lens at the sky, but before he could take a single shot there was a flash of white light and the thing was gone. The smell faded and a slight breeze kicked up, and Norman was left with a shaky but excited feeling.

He stared at the tree line, hoping to see the UFO return. The sky grew darker as he watched, and as more time passed he began to doubt his own perceptions, to wonder if what he had seen was a result of wishful imagining. He had been delving into the topic of aliens for a long time and believed in the possibility that an alien race with an interest in humanity could save humanity from itself. The star seed stalker had presented him with the very real possibility that Norman Jacobs as an individual may need to be rescued. As the dots made tenuous connections in his head, Norman's mood darkened.

He turned toward his car and walked briskly toward it, fighting the urge to look over his shoulder. He knew there was nothing hiding in wide open spaces around him.

The drive was uneventful, although there were no other cars on the road, which was odd. Usually, Norman passed a few other commuters going in the opposite direction even though the area was rural. He tried not to let his imagination get the best of him. Once home, he fought the urge to walk backwards to the front door, but let his paranoia get the better of him once the door was locked behind him. He left his keys and book by the front door and checked each room in the house, turning on every single light.

Norman went to the kitchen to make himself a cheese sandwich and open a bottle of wine. The interior of the house was a hash of classic masculine good taste and objects harkening to a boy's childhood dreams. On the leather couch lay a rumpled fuzzy blanket with stars and spaceships. An end table boasted a lamp in the shape of a flying saucer. Other objects of this nature were placed throughout the house. If a guest were to open a closed drawer he or she might find a stack of alien playing cards next to miniatures of creatures from mythology. Framed pictures of science fiction films and still shots from famous footage of Bigfoot and the moon landing hung on the walls where most people would have photos of family.

That's not to say that Norman did not have family photos around his home—they were just kept in the bedroom. Consciously, Norman thought he did this because he liked to have his family around in the place designated for rest; subconsciously, he believed they protected him from his own somewhat frightening areas of interest while he slept. Alien abduction fascinated him, but that did not mean he wished to experience the phenomena himself.

He situated himself on the couch and arranged his cheese sandwich, wine, and book on the coffee table in front of him. The wine bottle rested on a granite coaster with an etching of the Milky Way on it. He gathered his flying saucer blanket around himself for comfort and used the remote control to turn on the flatscreen TV which hung on the wall opposite him. It was already on the station which played classical music twenty-four hours a day. Norman was not a classical enthusiast, but he found that it was the perfect accompaniment to reading because it was wordless.

He took a bite out of his cheese sandwich and chased it with a large gulp of wine, then opened his book and began to read. Norman found the book fascinating, which distracted him from the creepiness of the star seed stalker and the concerns about his UFO sighting. This allowed the wine to do its slow but effective work of causing drowsiness. Norman fell asleep, the book slid from his lap, and spilled the star seed stalker's hand-hewn card onto the floor.

Norman's dreams were nonsensical, filled with amorphous shapes and blobs of color. Such dreams were common for him when he slept with the lights on.

The lights went off and the dreaming stopped. Whether it was the end of dreams, the sleeping brain's sudden perception of utter darkness, or a slight change of temperature that caused him to wake up with the hairs on the back of his neck standing up, he couldn't say.

The blackness was as startling to him as an explosion. For the first few seconds of being awake, he found himself unable to move, so that he was trapped staring into the dark. The house was too silent. An electrical hum usually hovered during times of quiet. It registered that the electricity must have gone out. It was not unusual for the electricity to go out in the middle of a storm, but the sound of rain pattering against the bedroom window was absent.

Norman thought maybe a truck hit a transformer somewhere, or perhaps he missed a notice for a scheduled blackout.

As he thought it through, his body loosened and he was able to move. He sat up and reached into the drawer of the end table. The flashlight was in the farthest corner causing Norman to stretch a little more than was comfortable. He let out a tiny grunt, which immediately made him feel self-conscious even though he was alone in the room. Once he had hold of the cylinder, he sat up properly, wincing as the couch groaned under his shifting weight. He pressed the button for on, but the light did not come on immediately. He shook the flashlight and heard the batteries inside knock against the confines of their plastic casing, and a soft round yellow glow appeared as a small dot on his blanket.

He swept the beam around the room as he waited for the beam to become stronger so that he could feel safe getting up. No aliens or ghosts lurked in the corners of his sanctuary. Norman stood. A bright white light flashed, flooding the room for a second. It blinked out and Norman suffered a red-orange after-image. It made him feel disoriented, off-balance.

He turned toward the window, which was closed, but the curtains and blinds had been left open. The white flash of light came again and lingered fractions of a second longer than the last time. Of course Norman thought of aliens, of the UFO he may or may not have seen earlier. His knees began to shake.

The beam of Norman's flashlight, now stronger, was aimed at the dark window. Two huge black eyes stared back at him, set in a stark gray face with a tiny mouth. Norman let out a startled cry. The apparition slanted its head to one side and seemed to consider Norman for a long time. There was a sort of notch at the visitor's temple.

Norman squinted, blinked, then opened his eyes a little wider, all in an attempt to see more clearly.

The notch, he saw, was not a notch at all, but rather a tiny hole through which an elastic band had been pulled. Whoever was staring at him through the window wore a mask, making it likely this was a human being than an E.T. The realization made Norman extremely angry. He strode to the window and yanked it open, shouting, "What the hell do you think you're doing?"

The "alien" he saw was of slight build and wore a zipped up black hooded sweatshirt, jeans, and red sneakers. The light had come from a flashlight the size of a bucket.

The intruder backed away from the window, but Norman reached out and snatched the cheap plastic mask from its head. He caught a glimpse of her—*her!*—face before she turned and ran, long red curly ponytail bouncing off into the night. What he saw of her face appeared human, but there was something wrong about the eyes that he hadn't enough time to figure out.

"I'm calling the cops!" he shouted after the retreating figure. He couldn't remember where his cell phone was, so he watched the woman run in the direction of the road in front of his house. She crossed the road and disappeared into a copse of trees.

He waited a bit longer, hoping to hear the sound of a vehicle starting up in the lonely night, but there was nothing. As he reached up to shut the window, his gaze was drawn to the sky. There was a cluster of stars just above the grouping of trees that seemed out of place, four bright stars hovering equidistant from one another. They wobbled slightly and then changed color, from white to purple. He blinked and they were gone.

He shook his head, closed and locked the window then searched the living room for his cell phone. He knew that the woman he saw had to be the star seed stalker; he also knew that he should not mention the weird blinking lights in the sky to the police. It had been so brief, he'd had wine, and it might have been some sort of optical trick because of all the light/dark contrasts with the flashlights, anyway. As he was on the phone explaining the situation to the police, the electricity switched on.

When the police came, they asked Norman to reiterate his story, dusted the window for fingerprints and examined the ground outside for footprints. The found a few prints but were not hopeful about leads. They agreed with him that his night time visitor and the star seed stalker could be the same person, but maybe not. "I mean, it's a small community and everyone knows what you do for a living," said one officer with a shrug. "It could just be some high school kids with a prank." They offered what sounded like standard precautions. Call the cops with any usual activity at the house or at work. Keep an incident journal. Keep the cell phone charged and ready at all times. They would make sure a patrol car drove by regularly.

Norman thanked them for all of their help. Although they hadn't done much except leave a mess of black powder on his window, he still felt safer knowing that the local authorities knew he was being harassed. He was certain that she would not be back that night. Norman returned to the couch and his book.

The arrival of dawn made Norman feel safe enough that he was able to fall asleep on the couch for a few hours.

He went to the station for work the next evening at 8 p.m. even though he wasn't meant to be on the air until midnight. It was a ritual for him. Four hours of show prep never quite seemed to be enough. His producer combed through pressing news stories that could become topics of discussion, but Norman also liked to do some of that research himself. He browsed the internet looking for news stories of the strange and unusual. It was like striking oil if he found a brand new story that happened to coincide with a guest's area of interest.

As soon as Norman walked into the studio his producer said, "I heard you had an interesting night last night."

"What?" Norman asked. He was slightly annoyed that Sam had stolen his thunder.

"It was on the local police blotter. I think you should mention it on the show," Sam suggested.

"Are you sure that's a good idea? She'll probably be listening. What if she does something worse the next time?"

Sam shrugged. "Well, maybe she'll call in and reveal her identity. Maybe it will get her to do something stupid so the authorities can deal with her."

Norman didn't have to think very long about it. Sam's ideas on the subject made sense. Norman also knew that he'd have a whole community of loyal listeners upset and concerned on his behalf. The locals would be alerted and maybe they could even help.

"Okay. I'll do it."

The guest for the night had cancelled because of a double-booking, so the plan was to air discussions with callers. Sam was still trying to get hold of one of the many psychics associated with the show. Norman loved the psychics. They usually made his job easy, and listeners were always interested.

Halfway through the show prep, Norman got extremely thirsty. "Hang on, Sam. I need to go get a drink."

"Okay. I'll see if any of our standbys got back to me yet."

Norman walked down the hallway to the lounge, headed for the soda machine. Usually, he opted for water because sometimes if he drank soda it made him burp, and that was extremely embarrassing on the air. Tonight, though, he had a craving for the crisp bite of carbonation.

Once inside the lounge, Norman felt something was wrong. It was colder than usual, and goose bumps rose on his arms. "I'm being paranoid," he muttered to himself. He reached into his right pocket for loose change and approached the machine, glancing at the "Hi Norman!" scratched into the front of the machine out of habit.

Placing the coins into the slot marked "Insert Coins Here," he then selected the button for cola and took a step back. The machine was notoriously fussy, sometimes taking a few minutes before the soda can dropped. Before the can fell, the machine always made a kind of muffled banging noise.

Norman didn't hear the expected bang. The machine kind of groaned, and at the end of the groan there was a high pitched whine. Something fell into the bin at the bottom of the machine, but it didn't sound like a soda can.

Norman furrowed his brow as he bent down to retrieve whatever happened to be in the bin. He touched something smooth and slippery. It pulsed and emitted a high pitched whine. His hand tingled as he pulled it away from the object. He knelt down and looked inside the bin. There was a small creature with the body of a human infant, except that its skin was gray. The head was larger than normal and it had two large black eyes that stared back at Norman, unblinking.

The tiny mouth twitched unnaturally and it squealed, reaching an arm toward him.

"Papa?"

Clover Forever

Addy Clover stood outside the Bronze Horse, half-watching the scene inside, her pale reflection superimposed over the frosty glass. At midnight, she would be turning twenty-one; she would be allowed inside to drink until her body told her to stop, or until 4 a.m., whichever happened to arrive first. Her mood hung somewhere between melancholy and anticipation. Being inexperienced with alcohol, she didn't know if booze would carry her to darkness or joy.

It doesn't matter as long as I look fabulous, Addy thought.

Her slightly older and more bar-savvy friend, Tom, hadn't arrived yet, which annoyed her. It was late, it was cold, and she felt just a little bit nervous about being a young woman standing alone in front of the entrance to a bar. It made her rethink her choice of clothing. Dark red lipstick, vintage heels, pencil skirt with fishnets. Her wig, which Addy had thought a chic and sophisticated bob, now made her feel like someone who had just stepped off a cabaret stage. The cold at the nape of her bare neck made her feel vulnerable, and not in an exciting, sexy way.

She glanced at her watch, then gazed past her reflection in the window. Polished brass and mahogany gave the bar a warm glow. High ceilings with slow-moving fans made it less claustrophobic than she had imagined it would be. The walls were painted a mottled orangey brown, making it homey. Addy approved. At least Tom hadn't chosen a dive for her first grown-up outing. She hoped this wouldn't also prove to be her last.

A booming voice called out behind her, "Doll-face! My god you look radiant! Chemo is doing wonders for your diet!"

Addy couldn't help but smile. Her last treatment had been a month ago, and she was in remission, but she wasn't about to spoil the mood by starting the night with medical jargon. Before she could turn around, Tom's big strong arms had enfolded her from behind. "Are you ready to go in, Birthday Girl?"

"I think so," Addy said. "Let's make this a night to remember."

They walked in and Tom started chatting with the bartender while Addy looked around the room.

She focused her attention on a tall blond man with a smooth complexion and rectangular black-rimmed glasses. He looked like he was trying to pick a fight.

"Oh my god!" Addy said. "That is the famous Scottish-American sculptor, Mack Taggert."

"Who?" Tom asked, then followed Addy's gaze to the other end of the bar. "Oh, that guy. I've met him. He's fun."

The bartender smirked. "You two should watch out for that guy. He's trouble."

Tom rolled his eyes, "He's an artist. How much trouble could he be? Addy, you should go talk to him."

Addy pulled away from Tom and turned to face him, placing her hands on her hips. "I think maybe you should buy me a drink first. This girl needs some liquid courage."

"It's a deal," Tom said.

Seductive jazz played over the speakers, mingling with the sound of ice being shaken inside a steel tumbler. Addy unzipped her coat and Tom helped her out of it, hanging it on a coat rack beside the door.

"Sara Silverstein sucks!" declared Taggert, loudly. "She stole my schtick! I've been doing potty humor since I was a two-year-old, and I didn't get famous for it!"

Addy tried not to look over as the sculptor's stockier companion laughed, then shook his head. "It's Silverman. And potty humor isn't the only thing she does."

Taggert lifted a shot glass to his lips, threw back his head, and let the rest of the amber liquid slide down his throat. "You're right, Jim, she also does me."

Jim chuckled like a dutiful sidekick.

The bartender refilled Taggert's shot glass, then turned to Addy and Tom, "What can I get you?"

Tugging Addy by the arm, Tom decisively responded, "Drinks!"

The bartender smiled, "Pull up a seat along the bar, Tom."

"Come on, Addy," Tom said as he sat on a stool. "Come sit next to your sugar daddy and let the bartender guess your drink."

Addy smiled and took her seat, beginning to relax as the earlier threat of a melancholy mood dissipated completely.

"Guess my drink?" Addy asked.

Tom grinned like a little boy showing off his favorite toy. "This guy is the master, and if I'm going to get you started on the road to alcoholism, then we ought to do it right."

The bartender winked at Tom. "Let's see." He crossed his arms in front of his chest while he pursed his lips, carefully considering Addy's appearance. "Very smooth and sophisticated, and yet, I sense this is a woman whose flower has yet to reach full bloom, eager for life. And yes, there it is, just a hint of fire."

Addy said, "You know I can hear you."

"Shush! Don't distract him, Addy, this is a serious art!" Tom said.

"Virgin at the bar!" Taggert yelled suddenly. The handful of people crowded at his end of the bar moved away slightly, shooting him alarmed looks. A few others laughed.

Addy felt her scalp turn crimson.

"Mack, back off, it's her twenty-first birthday," the bartender said.

"Like I said, virgin at the bar." Taggert sidled up to her. She stared at her purse. "So, I think I should give the birthday girl an orgasm."

"What?" Addy said, turning to face her antagonist. Tom was laughing. "And why are you laughing?"

"That's it!" exclaimed the bartender. "One Orgasm, coming right up."

"Hey, listen that's not—"

Taggert cut her short. He slapped her on the back and said to the bartender, "Can I call it or what?" He leaned in to Addy and said, "Come find me before you leave. I expect digits!"

Addy looked at Tom, who was still giggling.

"The look on your face is priceless."

"Did Mack Taggert just ask me for my phone number?" Addy whispered, incredulous.

The bartender set a creamy concoction in front of her with a smirk, "There's your Orgasm, sweetheart."

She stared at it for a moment, then started laughing. She downed the cocktail easily, and Tom congratulated her, offering to buy another drink. She opted for a light beer and a glass of water instead. As she and Tom drank and laughed, she could feel Taggert's presence in the bar. Addy could not deny that he held a certain appeal. Attractive and a little dangerous in a way she couldn't put her finger on. He was at the top of a profession that Addy admired. He was an artist, a person engaged in creating things beautiful and permanent, a person who would leave something behind that people might remember and appreciate for decades to come. She'd read the articles. His art was labeled transcendent by every critic. But that was all the information she had about him.

She kept saying to Tom, "I can't believe that guy is in here."

Tom said, "The crowd has thinned out. He's sitting over there by himself. You should go talk to him."

Addy sighed. "Buy me another drink first?"

"Okay, but you better not chicken out."

Addy's stomach felt weird, like it was turning upside down. "What if I pass out first?"

"Then I'll dump you on his lap. You two have been watching each other all night. This is a once-in-a-lifetime opportunity for misadventure."

Addy pursed her lips and steadied herself against the bar. "Peer pressure sucks."

Tom smiled, "Atta girl!"

Addy walked unsteadily toward the now red-faced Taggert, carrying a big glass of fruity drink Tom had supplied. Nervously, she took a seat next to Taggert.

Taggert leered, "Well, hello there."

"Hi," Addy replied. Her eyes sought Tom at the other end of the bar, but he was engaged in flirtation with the bartender.

"You're awfully quiet," Taggert said.

Addy shrugged and nervously tapped her feet on the brass ring on her stool, glad for its support. "I'm just shy."

He laughed. "I don't see how anyone who is shy can be friends with that guy."

"I'm not shy with him," Addy said, lifting the huge tumbler sip from, and hide her face. She gulped at it, eyeing Taggert over the rim, considering what to say.

He broke the silence first. "Is that a wig?"

Addy almost spit. "Yes."

"Why are you wearing a wig?"

She blinked. Her head was swimming, brain bereft of convincing lies. "Because I'm bald."

"Did you shave it off?" he asked.

"I had leukemia. I'm in remission," she blurted, turning the same strawberry hue as her drink.

Uncomfortable silence ensued.

Addy stood up. "I should go."

He hesitated. "No, don't go. What's a little cancer over drinks?"

The snarky comment reminded her of Tom. She hesitated.

"Besides, I'm just getting to know you," Taggert added.

That was much gentler. She slowly returned to her seat, but remained perched on the edge of it, ready to fly to Tom for rescue at the first sign of unpleasantness.

"That's better. Enough about you. Why don't you ask about me?"

She laughed nervously. "Modest aren't we?"

He smiled. "Not at all."

Addy stalled, searching her mind for questions. Art. She could start there. That would be easy.

"What made you choose art?"

Taggert shrugged. "I was good at it in grade school. I was encouraged. Plus I like working with my hands."

He held them out across the table, palms up. They were rough and calloused. Addy was used to the smooth, pink and pudgy hands of physicians. Made lean and rough by work, these hands were something new. Shaking, she reached out and traced their ridges with her fingers. Even as she did so, she was surprised at her own boldness, reminding herself that she was drunk and that tomorrow it would all be forgotten by everyone except herself.

Taggert sat quietly, allowing her to explore. Suddenly, he shivered. "Careful. You're gonna turn me on."

Addy's hands retreated, her face flushed. Art questions. She had to find something there.

"So, um, what about the idea of leaving something behind. When you make something that you know is amazing, does it feel like, by having made it, that your name will last forever?"

Taggert sat back, causing his coat fabric to whisper against wood. "That's an interesting question. It is kind of cool. Immortality and all of that. Very Greek pagan of you."

"Oh," she said, staring into her mug, wondering if her hands had calmed enough for her to lift it and drink.

"What about you, Addy? Would you like to leave something behind, so that you can be remembered forever?"

"Yes."

He smiled. "Then you should pose for me."

She shook her head. "I couldn't."

"Why not? You'd be my first angel."

"I'll think about it." She lifted her drink. She drank the rest of it down while Taggert ordered her another. Addy stared at the bartender. Beyond him at the end of the bar, Tom was giving her the thumbs up sign. She smiled at him, thinking, *Tom, I'm gonna kick your ass for this.*

"So you are interested in art, I take it," said Taggert.

"Yes."

"What's your favorite medium?"

She shrugged, "I gravitate towards painting. But I guess if I had to pick a favorite sculpture, it would be the classical Greek bronzes."

"Why?"

"I guess it's because they seem timeless. Bronze is strong, bold, durable. It kind of speaks to my imagination." She paused. "I probably sound like an idiot," she concluded, and stared at the back of her hands.

"I think you sound like a person who is thoughtful about what she likes."

Taggert and Addy locked eyes. Just as the length of silence between them began to grow more awkward, Tom bustled over.

"Looks like my chariot has arrived," she said, rising. She turned to Taggert. "It was nice getting to know you a little."

"Same here. Don't forget what I asked earlier. You should think about it," he said, sliding a folded napkin across the bar. Addy opened it, saw that it was his phone number. She stashed it into her purse.

Tom was just reaching them. "Think about what?"

"Becoming my sex slave," Taggert answered. "I'd pay her lots of money."

Tom's eyes widened in surprise and then narrowed in anger within a second.

Addy noticed the expression and was surprised by Tom's sudden protectiveness. "Tom, he's kidding. Let's go."

"What are you? Her pimp?" Taggert blurted. "We can deal."

Tom shook a finger at Taggert as Addy ushered him out the front door. She thought it felt colder outside than it had earlier, and shivered.

"Okay, Addy, please tell me again that he was kidding."

Addy grabbed Tom's hand and looked him in the eyes. "Tom, he was kidding."

"Okay. I believe you." He let out a sigh and unlocked the car doors. Addy got in. Tom started the engine and Addy waited until he got out of the parking space to ask, "What's gotten into you anyway? I thought you liked him."

Tom glanced over at her. "I don't know. I heard some things."

"Between getting to the bar and leaving it?"

Tom laughed, wryly. "No. Before that. He's not a nice man."

Addy quietly said. "That doesn't mean he's not a good man, Tom. You know that."

"I know." Tom paused. "Do you think he's a good man, Addy?"

"I don't know yet."

The sound of the motor running and the whoosh of passing traffic filled the car while the two gathered their thoughts. Tom broke the silence, "So what did he ask you?"

"He asked if I would pose for him."

Tom's whole face brightened, "Addy that's awesome! I think you should do it."

"What? Two seconds ago you were all like, 'I heard some things' and now you think I should spend more time with the guy?"

Tom shrugged, "It's different, now that I know what he actually asked you. Think of it, Addy, you'll be famous, like the way the mysterious Mona Lisa is famous. How cool is that?"

She lifted her chin, "Well I don't know if I'm gonna do it. You said he's not a nice man."

"Shut up," he said, throwing a balled-up glove at her head. "You'll do it. Besides, I'm not always a nice man either. Do you remember how we met?"

She grinned, "How could I forget?"

Addy had met Tom when she was five and he was seven, in the children's cancer ward at St. Patrick's Hospital. They were on the same treatment schedule, so their paths always crossed. They never spoke to each other until one day in the playroom Addy found a bright purple ball with little unicorns painted across its equator. She was fascinated by it, so she grabbed it and took it with her into a quiet corner to stare at it. She named all the unicorns. To Addy, the ball was a bright spot of colorful magic in her otherwise bland world. Who cared about lettered blocks and puzzles when you had a whole herd of unicorns to look after?

Tom noticed her with the ball and decided that he wanted it, too. With a herculean effort, he wheeled over to Addy's corner and bumped her with his chair, knocking the ball out of her hands. Addy, too surprised to cry, looked up at him, her mouth in a perfect little O. Panting from exertion, he said, in his tinny little boy's voice, "Bitch, that's my ball."

Addy was just about to ask him what the word meant, because she'd never heard it before, when he turned his chair and went toward the ball. It had rolled under a regular chair, so he had to lower himself out of the wheelchair to get it. In the time it took for Tom to do that, Addy had reached the same spot, and they both went under the chair, weakly kicking and scratching at each other to get to the ball. Addy imagined that the fight must have looked like two lazily flopping fish, but at the time, they both felt like they were as dynamic as action heroes. By the time they were rescued from each other, instead of being upset, they were both giggling hysterically. In that moment, they became best friends. All the well-meaning doctors, nurses, and parents couldn't keep them apart. Tom became Addy's bright spot of magic, and she became the same for him.

She felt nervous as they pulled into her driveway, not wanting to tell Mom about Taggert, but not wanting to lie to her either. She was still a little drunk, and Tom told her that she needed to eat and have some coffee and water before falling asleep, or she would regret it later.

They got out of the car in silence and slowly trudged up to the house. As they approached the door, Addy was surprised at how tired she felt from the evening's excursion, and reached for Tom's arm as her feet struggled to find traction on the ice.

Addy's mom, Babs, waited for them by the door, wearing an overlong cardigan. Her gray-streaked hair was in a ponytail and she wore red-rimmed reading glasses. Addy winced at the sight of those reading glasses. She hated them because they reminded her that her mother was aging. Addy was used to being confronted with her own mortality but she couldn't bear seeing signs of it in the people she cared about.

They entered and Addy looked sheepish, keeping her head low and trying not to make eye contact with her mother. Tom took the opposite approach and greeted her with a mischievous grin and an aggressive hug.

Babs rolled her eyes at Tom during the embrace, and wagged her finger disapprovingly as he stepped away. Her mouth betrayed her, though: Addy noticed one side was quirked upwards in a half smile, barely suppressed. The smile remained even as Babs placed her hands on her hips and said, "You kept Addy out much longer than you were supposed to. I hope you are proud of yourself, Thomas."

Tom bowed at the waist, then stood up. "Always."

Mom shook her head. "You are incorrigible."

"Don't forget to feed her, now, Babs. Well, I should get going." He winked at Addy. "My job here is done."

Addy smiled. "Thanks, Tom."

"Anything for you, Princess." Tom closed the door behind him.

Mom turned to her and said, "It's a shame that boy is gay. He really loves you."

Addy smiled, "Yeah, I know." Her stomach rumbled.

"Okay, kid, let's get you some food."

She followed her mother into the kitchen, which was full of good food smells that turned out to be baked potato and pasta.

"Tom said you'd be needing starches to soak up the alcohol." Mom placed a huge dish in front of her at the kitchen table and sat down opposite with a steaming cup of tea. She took off her reading glasses and set them aside.

Addy loaded her fork with pasta and shoved it in her mouth. It was dressed with butter and salt, only, but it tasted like a miracle.

"So, tell me about your night," Mom said.

Addy almost spat out her food. She'd thought she'd managed to avoid having to let her mom know about Taggert. She blushed, all the way through her scalp. "There's not much to tell. I met someone interesting. A sculptor."

"Okay," Mom said, "So, tell me about him."

There was a beat of silence while Addy struggled with what to tell her mother. "He asked me to pose for him," she said quietly.

"What are you talking about?"

Addy lifted her chin defiantly. "He's a sculptor. A famous one, Mom, and he wants me to pose for him."

Mom shook her head. "I don't like it. We don't know anything about this man. What's his name?"

"Mack Taggert. He says I'll be his first angel."

"Addy, I don't know about this," said Mom. "He doesn't mean nude, does he?"

Addy hadn't thought of that, but from what she had seen of his work, he never did nudes.

"Tom thinks I should do it."

Mom laughed bitterly. "Tom. You know, sometimes I don't know if he's always the best influence on you. I still have nightmares about those bruises you got from him the day you met."

Addy hadn't been sure before this whether or not to say yes to Mack's proposal. She understood her mother's point of view, and there were things about him that made her feel hesitant. Stronger than both of those factors was her love of art. When the cancer was at its worst and Addy could not even focus enough to follow the storyline in a television program, couldn't concentrate enough to read a book, she could always find solace in paintings. They demanded nothing of her other than appreciation. And when she was feeling better, she could revisit them, interpret, analyze, absorb information about the artists, discover what story the picture's thousand words tried to tell. She did not have the gift to make her own, but by posing for Mack, she could become a vital part of just one piece of that which had fed her soul during her long years of struggling with cancer. Tom was right. She was going to do it.

"Mom, it's a chance for me to be a part of something bigger than myself."

Mom poured coffee into her mug and shuffled toward the table, looking at Addy with pleading eyes.

"I just don't want you to get hurt. Artists are always bad news for young girls like you."

"How do you know that?" she asked. Her mother did not answer. She ventured forward. "The cancer has made my world so small. This is a chance to make it larger."

Mrs. Clover's face looked pale, old and sad. "I still don't like it. I want you to experience the world, I really do. I just want you to be safe."

Addy picked up her fork and listlessly shifted the food on her plate. Suddenly, an idea popped into her head. "Then come with me."

Mom took a sip of her coffee. "What?"

"Come with me. You can chaperone. He's not going to do anything crazy if you're there, and if he does, it'll be over. But I'll have had my chance."

"Honey, I have to work."

"So? Then Tom can chaperone. Please? Just think about it."

Mrs. Clover sighed. "Okay."

A few days later, Addy phoned Taggert and said yes, she'd pose, but only with a chaperone. On the other end of the phone, he laughed. "Okay, but make sure Mom brings a book or something. It's gonna be boring for her. And bring whatever else you think you'll need. Water. Music. Whatever."

"How long is a session?"

He paused, "It depends. I use a few different techniques to study the subject. Sometimes it's only an hour or two, sometimes five."

"Okay."

That Saturday morning, Addy arrived, with her mother, at Mack's studio. They let themselves in, as he'd instructed. Addy could tell that her mother was relieved to find that the studio did not double as his apartment. There was a bathroom, of course, a coffee-maker, a microwave, and a mini-fridge, but no signs that he slept there. There was also no sign of Taggert. They waited expectantly by the door for a moment before Addy decided to explore.

The place was huge, the first floor of an abandoned factory lined on all four sides with immaculately clean windows. It was like walking into a dream. In one corner, there were large vats for the casting of metal. There was a traditional kiln for ceramics, and multiple shelves laden with tools for sculpting, chipping and shaping. Blocks of wood and stone were scattered haphazardly in different areas, as likely to show up next to the workbench as near the mini-fridge. Black canvas covered some of the windows, and Addy noticed it was rolled above all of them, unique blinds meant to control the amount of light let in.

In the easternmost corner was what Addy thought of as the staging area. Blindingly white sunlight poured in through the windows behind a block of wood covered by a fluffy white rug. In front of that was an easel, replete with sketch pad, and a small round table that looked like it had been painted by a child. On top of the table were a few charcoal pencils and a digital camera. There was a small area closed off by folding screens which Addy could only guess was to be her changing room. She swallowed, wondering what outrageous costume Mack had devised for an angel to wear.

A folding chair was set near the easel, next to another small round table and a milk crate with a well-worn seat cushion on top of it. There were a few space heaters nearby as well. Addy turned to it with a smile on her lips. "Well, Mom, I guess this is your throne."

Mrs. Clover wasn't looking at the chair. She was gazing at equipment in the darkened corner. "Addy, do you know what all this stuff is?"

She shrugged, "Some of it. I've seen it in my art books."

Mrs. Clover walked toward Addy and the chair that had been so carefully arranged for her. She laid her bag down on it, unzipped her coat, and began unpacking the supplies she'd brought with her: a six-pack of bottled water, a bag of cherries, a few sandwiches made with wholly organic ingredients. Finally, she drew out the suggested book and some of Addy's CDs. She took off her winter coat halfway, shivered, and then slid it back on.

"I'm turning the space heater on. I'm not waiting for Mr. Taggert to show up."

Addy winced at her mom's derisive inflection on Mack's name. She hoped that it wouldn't go badly between them.

At that moment, Mack bustled through the front door, bearing two cardboard trays with eight large coffees.

"Sorry I'm late. I was here earlier to get set up and realized I didn't have any coffee, and the stuff I make for myself is pretty gross."

He set the coffees on top of the mini-fridge and said, "Help yourselves," as he took off his coat.

Addy's mother stood with her hands on her hips. "There's nothing extra in that coffee, is there?"

Addy groaned inwardly, wishing her mother wasn't so paranoid. It was embarrassing. Mack stopped his bustling movements, a steaming cup of coffee in hand, and said, "Madame, I assure you, I never imbibe while I'm working."

A smile played on Mack's face as he walked toward Addy's mother. Addy couldn't tell if he was amused or irritated. "See for yourself," he said, handing the coffee to Mrs. Clover.

She removed the plastic lid and sniffed at the coffee, then hesitantly took a sip. Addy's heart pounded in her chest while she watched. As Mrs. Clover's attention was on the coffee, Mack quickly winked at Addy. It did not comfort her.

Mrs. Clover sighed. Addy couldn't tell if it was relief or if she'd been hoping to find a reason to whisk Addy away before the session began. Whichever it was, she found no alcohol in the coffee. She replaced the lid and handed it back to him.

"Nice to meet you, Mr. Taggert."

Mack gave her a slight bow and said, "It's an honor, Mrs. Clover."

He lifted another cup of coffee out of the tray and brought it over to Addy while Mrs. Clover got one for herself. He set his own coffee down on his work table and clasped his hands together. "Well, Addy, are you ready?"

Addy blinked. "I think so."

"I'll take your coat."

"Thank you."

Mack draped her coat over the corner of one of the screens set up as a dressing room. He turned to Addy's mom. "I'll take yours, too, if you like, Mrs. Clover."

"It's cold in here."

Addy was wearing white long johns with some baggy shorts over them. Mack had requested that she wear white. He gave her the once-over, which made Addy blush and Mrs. Clover bristle. Addy leaned down to remove her boots but he stopped her.

"No. Leave the boots, I think. But you'll want to get rid of the shorts and the wig."

Mrs. Clover opened her mouth as if to protest but Mack quickly added, "There's a white skirt behind those screens."

Addy touched her wig, self-consciously. "I thought it would be better with the wig."

Mack shook his head and gestured to the screens.

Addy silently went behind them. The room was so quiet she could hear her mother's weight shifting in the chair and Mack's preparations. The silence made her uneasy. She took off her shorts and called out. "Can you guys put on some music or something?"

"You got it," Mack called out.

As Addy found the huge flowing white skirt and put it on, she heard the strains of familiar music fluttering through the room. It was one of the mixed CDs that she'd brought with her. She smiled, feeling more relaxed now that the room was flooded with sound.

She emerged from the dressing room wigless and bathed in white.

"So when do I get my wings?"

"Not yet," said Mack. "I have to figure out what's going to look most natural first."

Mrs. Clover let out a little disapproving, "Hmm," but didn't say anything. Addy shot her a warning look.

"Okay, Addy, up you go."

She took her place on the wood block and let him pose her. She stood facing the easel, her head turned in three-quarter profile looking down toward her right hand, outstretched to the left, palm up. The sun's rays streaming through the windows warmed her back. She was nervous for the first few minutes, not used to being studied.

Mack started with the digital camera, taking hundreds of shots from every angle. He was quiet and had a serious expression on his face as he worked. The only things he said were instructions to Addy to lift her chin, lean to the left, adjust the position of her shoulders. This diligent, focused side of him was very different from what she knew of him so far. She hadn't known what to expect, but was convinced that Tom's advice to take up the invitation was right.

About an hour and a half into the session, he finally pronounced it to be break time. Addy was surprised to find herself sore from standing in the same position for so long. She stretched and yawned. Mack approached and offered her the support of his arm to help her down off the block.

Mrs. Clover had fallen asleep in the chair, her feet propped up on the milk crate, and her book had fallen to the floor.

Addy and Mack looked at each other and smiled. They'd won a few moments away from Mrs. Clover's watchful gaze.

They walked toward the mini-fridge together, Addy had her cold coffee in hand and drank it down greedily.

"I didn't realize how hungry and thirsty I was getting until just now."

"I get like that every time I work. I lose track of time and forget about that stuff."

Addy reached into the mini-fridge for her sandwich. She unwrapped it and took a huge bite. After she'd swallowed she turned to Mack, who was heating up some Ramen noodles, and said, "Thank you for inviting me to be a part of this."

He raised an eyebrow. "I should be thanking you. You sure you aren't getting bored up there?"

"No," Addy said, taking another bite of sandwich. Talking with her mouth full, she added, "The music helps."

The microwave buzzed, letting Mack know his mid-morning lunch was ready.

Mrs. Clover woke with a start and her foot dropped off the milk crate, which caused it to scrape across the floor. The sound warned Addy and Mack and they jumped away from each other a little, as if they had been doing something wrong.

"What time is it?" said Mrs. Clover.

"It's about ten-thirty," said Mack.

Mrs. Clover blinked. "What are you doing, eating lunch? Is there any coffee left?"

Mack quirked an eyebrow at Addy. "Is she always this inquisitive when she wakes up?"

Addy giggled, "Yes."

Mrs. Clover yawned and stood up then joined Addy and Mack over their meal. She unwrapped her own sandwich and started eating while Mack and Addy finished theirs.

"So, Mr. Taggert, can I ask you a question?" Mrs. Clover said.

"Sure."

"Why all the photography first?"

"The answer's not very interesting."

"Indulge me."

"Well, what I do is take digital photos from every angle I can, then download them into a computer program that compiles all the images to make a three-dimensional model that I can work from," he explained.

"Where's the advantage in that?" Addy asked.

Mack grinned. "Well, that way I can choose multiple poses for a live model and then see how those poses might work as a sculpted piece, and make a decision about which one to use."

"What about spontaneity? Or Michelangelo's idea that when you carve something out of stone or wood, your job is to release the image within?"

Mrs. Clover looked at Addy with wide eyes as Mack answered. "I believe that even he had an idea of what image he was creating before he put the chisel to David's marble. And of course there are variations in detail as you get into the project. It's never perfectly aligned to the image you start with. The digital medium just gives me more choices and eliminates some of the trial and error. And of course, once the image is chosen, it goes back to the more organic process of using your hands to learn the lines of the subject."

Mrs. Clover's eyes narrowed in sudden suspicion.

Addy rolled her eyes, "Mom, he's talking about the sketch pad. He sketches to learn the lines before making the mold or doing the carving."

Mack crossed his arms and looked at Mrs. Clover. "Wow, Addy, your Mom has a dirty mind."

Mrs. Clover cleared her throat, "I'm sorry." She excused herself to go to the bathroom as Mack and Addy cleaned up after lunch. When she emerged, Mack and Addy were already working again.

The rest of the session passed uneventfully, after which Mrs. Clover agreed that Mack, at least while he was working, seemed safe enough for Addy be with.

"But never without a chaperone!" she added in the car on the way home. "Although I'm willing to let Tom go with you next time."

Addy invited Tom over as soon as she got home. She didn't want to talk about the session within Mom's earshot, so they went for a walk.

"So, how was it?" Tom asked.

Addy shrugged, teasing him by playing up her nonchalance. "What's to tell? I posed, he took pictures. End of story."

"Oh, come on!"

"Okay, okay!" Addy said. "It was pretty awesome."

"So how did Babs take it?"

Addy laughed and told him about how tense her mom was, and how Mack surprised her by being quiet and serious for most of the session.

"There really aren't a whole lot of fireworks to report," Addy said. "I just know that it felt really cool to be a part of something like that. Although, there is one interesting thing."

"What's that?"

"Mom said she'd let you chaperone next time."

Tom's eyes widened, "Are you serious? How did you manage that?"

Addy laughed. "I think she was bored. She fell asleep. You'll probably be bored, too."

"Not a chance. You see, unlike your overprotective mother, I won't feel compelled to stay there the entire time."

"Oh, I see how it is!"

Suddenly Addy felt something warm and wet on her upper lip and she felt dizzy. She stumbled forward slightly, but Tom caught her.

"Hey, Addy. Are you okay?"

She noticed fresh drops of blood on the snow. "I think my nose is bleeding."

Tom's voice was full of alarm. "Shit. Here, take my arm."

Addy felt weak. "Tom, I don't feel so good."

Tom reached into his pocket with his free hand and retrieved an unopened packet of tissues. He handed them to Addy.

"Let's find a bench. It's probably nothing major. Just too long of a day, that's all. Doctors said it would take a while before you started to have a normal energy level."

Addy only half-heard Tom's reassurances. All she knew was that her body was suddenly failing her, again. He might be right—normal people with decent health got nosebleeds all the time. It didn't necessarily mean the cancer was back. She had a check-up in a few days anyway, so there was no reason to panic yet.

Tom ushered her over to a bench and made her tilt her head back and apply pressure to the bleed.

Addy was exhausted for the next few days, and spent most of her time in bed, reading her art books and daydreaming about the sculpture Mack was going to create. She made sure to keep her energy up around her Mom, not wanting to worry her. It seemed to work.

The day of the doctor's appointment came. Addy was quiet, subdued. Her mother couldn't help noticing.

In the waiting room, Mom finally asked, "Addy are you okay?"

"I'm just nervous."

Addy's mother swallowed and glanced over at her but didn't say anything.

Addy knew that her mother shared her fears, and just like Addy, she was doing her best to keep up a calm front. It was the first time at a medical appointment that Addy asked her mother not to go into the room with her.

The doctor asked her how she was feeling. She admitted to the fatigue and the nosebleed. He said that it might just be part of recovery, but his eyes belied concern as he said, "But I'm going to draw some blood just to be safe." He took her vitals, felt the glands in her neck. His brow furrowed and Addy knew he'd come across something. She felt her throat begin to close as despair welled up inside her. She didn't want to be sick again. She'd spent her whole life fighting and she was too tired.

When Addy emerged from the office to meet her mother in the waiting room, she was pale and shaking.

"Addy?"

"I can't talk now. Let's just go," she said hoarsely. She didn't look at her mother, just kept walking out the front door while her mother rushed after her.

"Addy!" Mrs. Clover called after her, struggling to get her coat on. She caught up to Addy near the car and gently touched her shoulder.

"Honey?"

The sobs welled up from deep within and burst forth like a broken dam, and Addy clung to her mother like a life raft.

"Oh, baby girl," Addy's mom whispered hoarsely through her own tears.

A few days later, the results were in, and they said what Addy knew they would. The doctor wanted to talk to her about treatment options. Addy told her mother to handle it, she just wasn't strong enough.

They were quiet with each other the rest of the week, each knowing that a word or gesture was likely to set the other off in a crying fit. Then Saturday rolled around and Tom arrived to take Addy to Mack's studio. She had forgotten.

Tom's face was grim when he arrived at the door.

"Addy, what's going on? I haven't heard from you all week! Are we still doing this today? Mack said he kept trying to reach you."

"I'm sorry Tom, I forgot."

Tom looked at her pale face and knew what was wrong, and in typical Tom fashion, he blurted, "Addy, are you sick again?"

She nodded.

"Fuck," he muttered.

Addy thought she was going to cry again, but surprised herself by laughing. "You said it, Tom."

"Can I at least come in out of the cold?"

"Yeah. Let's go to my room."

Tom took the invitation.

Addy sat on her bed, as did Tom. He glanced at the art book lying open next to her pillow, alongside a pile of used tissues and half-empty bottles of water.

The two friends paused for a moment, just looking at each other with fond smiles, until Tom broke the silence, "Addy, this is starting to turn into a Sam and Frodo moment."

She laughed. "We don't want that. Peter Jackson might sue."

He grinned. "Mack's waiting. We should call him if you aren't up to it today. But—"

"But you think I should go anyway." Addy looked at her pile of tissues and open art book.

"I'm gonna be blunt here, Addy—"

"When are you anything but?"

Tom rolled his eyes. "If you are going to die, don't you think you owe it to yourself to see this through?"

"Fuck you, Tom," she said, but there wasn't any real anger behind her words. She'd already been thinking that this time she might not make it. She'd already been considering that it might be best to forgo treatment and just live the rest of her too-short life comfortably at home with her Mom, surrounded by the things she loved.

Tom took her mild outburst in stride. "Addy, I love you. I'm not going to let you throw away an opportunity to do something that I know makes you happy just because you might be dying."

Addy drew up her legs and hugged her knees. "You mean that exactly because I might die, I need to do this."

Tom nodded, "It's your chance to shine before your light goes out."

Addy sighed, then grinned wickedly, "Before I kick the bucket."

"Before you're six feet under."

"Before I meet my maker."

"Before you're worm food."

"Before its time to take a dirt nap."

"That's my girl," Tom said. "You know dirt nap is my favorite."

Tom's cell phone rang. He looked at the caller ID and showed Addy.

"It's Mack. Should I take it?"

Addy nodded, then got up off the bed and started getting dressed.

Before they left, Addy asked Tom to shave her head.

"This time, I want it to be by choice."

Tom smiled, "You do have an exceptionally attractive skull."

Addy and Tom arrived at Mack's with three bags of junk food, a carton of cigarettes, and a dime bag.

"Addy! Love of my life! I thought you'd never get here!" Mack said as he approached with open arms.

Tom immediately interposed himself between Mack and Addy, holding out their grocery bags. Mack stuck out his tongue at him, then the three went over to the makeshift kitchen. Tom started emptying the bags. Soda, chips and dip, chocolate, some microwave burgers, all went to their proper place. When Tom was done with the emptying, he tossed the dime bag over to Mack.

"Here. That should make everyone feel better."

Mack looked at the bag in surprise, "Nice! I didn't think you two smoked."

"We don't. But Addy has new orders from Doctor Tom."

"I do?" Addy asked.

"Yes. Until the big dirt nap, you have to do something every day that you've never done before. We're gonna squeeze as much life into the time you've got left as we can."

"Do they all have to be illegal?" Addy asked.

"Of course not!" Tom said, "Just half of them."

"What are you talking about?" asked Mack.

Leave it to Tom to start the conversation on a high note, Addy thought. "I'm sick again."

Mack blinked and took a step back. "Um, I have to go to the bathroom."

The bathroom wasn't that far away so Addy and Tom could hear him muttering to himself in there. Addy decided to put some music on to help cover up the sound and give Mack some privacy.

While she did that, Tom prepared Addy's breakfast: a bottle of coke and a plate of chocolate.

"I can't eat that for breakfast!" she protested.

"Ah, but you've never eaten chocolate for breakfast. This is part one of Doctor Tom's regimen."

"But—"

"But what? It's bad for the big C?"

"Well, yeah," Addy said.

Tom put his hands on her shoulders and looked into her eyes. "Doctor Tom says it is high time you started laughing in the face of the Big C. Say it with me. I laugh..."

Addy grinned and joined him with a melodramatic flourish, "I laugh in the face of the Big C!"

"Very good. So it's chocolate for breakfast. And later, you shall try your very first cigarette."

Addy wrinkled her nose, "Ew. Are you trying to torture me?"

"Doctor Tom is just getting you caught up with what every other normal person has experienced at least once."

"And you think you're the poster child of normal?"

"Shut up and eat your chocolate."

She dutifully followed Doctor Tom's orders. Chocolate for breakfast was divine. She hoped he'd forget about the cigarettes.

Mack was in the bathroom for a long time. Addy was mildly concerned for him. It was clear he didn't know how to handle the news. Tom hadn't chosen the gentlest way of breaking it to him, but maybe it was better to get it out of the way. When he finally came out, his eyes were red-rimmed and he was followed by a giant cloud of marijuana smoke.

Addy inhaled some of it and started coughing. She and Tom started talking simultaneously. Addy said, "I thought you never imbibed while you're working?"

Tom said, "You better not have smoked all of it!"

Mack looked at them both resentfully. "I thought today might be a good time to make an exception. And no. I didn't smoke all of it."

Mack brushed past them and walked over to the easel. "Okay, let's get started."

Addy ran her hands over her smooth skull.

"How do you want me?"

Mack snapped, "I don't know. Have Tom pick a pose."

Tom and Addy looked at each other and quietly got down to the business of picking a pose. Tom had Addy kneel in a crouch on the wooden block and look down. "Thought we should start with a tough one first." He played with the skirt, getting the folds to lie in a way that he thought pleasing.

"Tom, that tickles."

"Stop fucking around!" Mack barked.

Tom put his hands up, "Okay." He backed away and addressed Addy. "I'm going out for a walk. You can deal with Captain Surly."

Mack picked up a charcoal pencil and threw it at Tom, but his aim was wild and he missed him by a wide arc. He worked much more quickly this time, his movements efficient as he snapped away furiously. When he was finished with the camera, Addy asked, "Are we done with this one?"

"No. Stay there."

Addy silently obeyed. She felt overwhelmed by sadness as he took up the sketchbook and began drawing as furiously as he had taken the photos. Addy suddenly had visions of herself painted as the angel of death. No shine there, just the darkness of grief. And there was Mack with his premature grief, in the form of anger. Addy hadn't realized that it would affect him this much—they barely knew each other. Silently, she started to cry.

Mack continued sketching, his movements slowly became less hurried, more steady and calm. The work itself seemed to give him what he needed to cope. As he grew calmer, so did Addy. It wasn't long before she heard him softly call her name.

"You can get down now."

Addy got down off the block and sat on it, staring at her feet.

Mack walked over to her and said her name again, softly. She kept staring at her feet, not wanting to look up at him and see anger, or grief. She knew she'd break down if she had to bear his sadness as well as her own. As he drew closer, Addy noticed that the smell of marijuana clung to him like a shroud.

"Addy," he whispered, cupping her chin in his hand, gently forcing her face up toward him. His eyes were full of earnestness. "I don't want you to go."

He kissed her with unexpected softness and she closed her eyes and melted into it, feeling warmth flood her body.

A gust of cold air suddenly filled the room. Mack reluctantly pulled away and looked toward the door. Tom stood in the doorframe, looking at Addy with a question in his eyes.

"Well, that must have been some kiss."

Addy tried to play dumb, "What kiss?"

"Don't give me that," Tom reprimanded. He hurried over to Addy, digging in his coat pocket. "Your nose is bleeding."

Addy raised her hand to her upper lip. She drew it away and saw bright red blood glistening on her fingers.

"Tilt your head back." As Tom ministered to Addy's nosebleed, Mack took a pack of cigarettes from the carton and lit one up.

"I think you win a free pass on the cigarettes today, Addy," Tom said.

"Thank you, Doctor Tom." Addy's voice was muffled by the tissue held up to her nose.

Tom shrugged. "I think first kiss trumps first cigarette."

"Okay, I didn't want to know that," Mack said.

"Why?"

"Because now I feel guilty."

"Don't be so friggin Catholic," Tom said.

Addy laughed and immediately regretted it, because it increased the pressure in her nose. "Ow."

"Great, now she's laughing at me." Mack shook his head and took another deep drag on the cigarette. "I'm going for a walk. You guys can play with the camera if you want."

"Oooh!" said Tom. "Let's take some hot pictures of your nosebleed Addy. To commemorate the nosebleed kiss."

"Tom! Stop making me laugh!"

The door slammed shut behind Mack.

As soon as he was gone, Tom took up the camera and started snapping pictures. Addy threw her bloody tissue at him and then laid down on the block, but he kept taking pictures.

"Tom, stop that and go get me some food. I'm starving, and exhausted."

He looked at the last picture he'd snapped. "You're right. That last one is really morbid."

"Let me see," Addy demanded.

"No. I have to go get your food. You said you were starving."

Tom took the camera with him to the kitchen, leaving her to stare at the ceiling.

She really was exhausted. Bone tired. Her knees ached, there was a dull throb in her head, and her limbs felt like they were weighted down with lead. It was only going to get worse with another round of chemotherapy. She didn't want to go through that again. But as awful as she felt, she was happy. She was doing something she never thought she'd do.

"Tom?"

"Yeah?"

She looked up where the steel crossbeams intersected then closed her eyes. "I think I want to go out on a high note."

Tom burned his finger on a freshly-microwaved burger. "Ow! Addy, what are you talking about?"

"I want to leave the party while I'm still having a good time."

Tom cleared his throat and walked over to her, carrying burgers and sodas. He sat down next to her on the block. "Addy, I know you'd never usually hear me say this, but please stop talking in euphemisms and tell me exactly what you mean by that."

Addy sat up and took a bite out of her burger. She chewed slowly. Tom waited her out, not saying a word. Finally, she swallowed.

"No more treatment. It's a miracle I've made it this far."

Tom looked away from her. "I had a feeling it was something like that."

"There's something else," Addy said.

"What else could there be? Like watching you go through this without fighting isn't going to be hard enough!"

"I thought you'd understand."

"I do understand, Addy. That doesn't make it less painful."

She looked at Tom thoughtfully. "We'll talk about it later. Right now I need food and a nap."

"Okay."

They finished their meal in silence, and Addy curled up on the wood block and fell asleep.

She woke to see that the warehouse had grown dark. Someone had thrown a worn old blanket over her. Tom and Mack had opened a bottle of wine and were talking in hushed tones. She got up and stretched, feeling some physical relief from her fatigue. She walked over to the easel to see a fully-developed sketch of herself sleeping. The figure didn't look sick in the sketch, just bald.

Addy turned from the easel toward the boys.

"Morning, sunshine!" said Mack.

"Hi. How long was I out?"

Tom shrugged, "A couple of hours. Don't worry. I called Babs. I told her we might end up being here all night."

"Is there any coffee?" she asked.

"I thought you might ask that," said Mack. "We went out. There's a couple in the tray right here."

She walked over to the coffee. There was a large black shopping bag resting against the mini-fridge.

"What's that?"

"Got you something," Tom said.

Mack reached into the bag and pulled out a pair of fluffy white wings.

Addy grinned. "Can I try them on?"

Tom and Mack strapped her in. The wings felt strange and heavy, and pulled on her lower back, but she loved them anyway.

"Are we gonna go again?" Addy asked, expectantly.

Mack shrugged, "If you feel up to it. I don't want to push you."

Tom piped in. "I think it's a bad idea."

Addy pouted, "I've slept for an age! I have energy now, so I think we should do it."

"Okay, but the second you get tired again, we're going."

Addy floated back to the wooden block.

The next few weeks passed in a haze for Addy. Her energy gradually deteriorated and shadows began to appear under her eyes, shadows that could not be wiped away by sleep. She experienced incredible surges of happiness when she was in the studio; and when she was away from it, she sank into despair, the angel coming down to Earth. She tried to hide it from her mother, who worried over her incessantly. Sometimes, Addy heard her mother crying at night, unable to bear the idea that Addy simply would not fight. There was no hope of hiding it from Mack and Tom.

All the while, she had one thought, *I want to be bronzed before I die.*

Since the kiss, Tom would not leave Addy alone in the studio with Mack; until one day, when they ran out of coffee and bottled water, he offered to go to the store. As soon as the door had closed behind Tom, Mack said, "So, Addy, if I kiss you again, will it hurt?"

Addy smiled, "Dying girls still like kisses."

Mack frowned, "I wish you wouldn't say things like that."

"Then forget I said it and come here."

It was soft and lingering, but Addy wanted more. Timidly, she pulled him closer. His calloused hands slipped under her shirt, tracing soft patterns on the fragile skin of her back. Up until that moment, Addy's sighs had always been of resignation, sadness, disgust; this was her first sigh of pleasure. She wanted more. Gently, with her arms, legs, and mouth, she urged Mack to give those sighs to her.

The first hush of skin against skin made her shiver; then heat grew between them and she felt transported, enveloped in a soft cocoon where no pain could reach her.

The shock of his entry made her cry out in pain. Her eyes opened and raked around the room; the lights, the makeshift dressing room, her wings on the bare concrete floor, a pool of spilled water. The pain subsided, and she calmed as he rocked her gently with his movements, the rhythm of his breathing. Her eyes settled on the warm pink skin of his neck and shoulder; she watched a single trickle of sweat make its lonely path from behind his ear and down his neck, finally disappearing into the space between them, the space she could not see. Addy wanted to stay inside that moment forever.

When Mack pulled away, his hand brushed her cheek and he searched her face. "Are you okay?"

"I'm more than okay."

"Tom's gonna be back soon."

"Shush, don't let that spoil this."

He smiled, kissed her forehead, and then pulled up his pants. Addy quickly got dressed, a strange feeling lingering between her legs. As if he'd left some sort of mark on this previously untouched part of her. A fleeting thought occurred to Addy, that if she wasn't a dying girl, this would be the moment to experience regret. But there was no time for that, and she had to ask him to do something for her. Something difficult...

"Mack?" She reached out to touch his arm.

"Yes?"

"I need you to do something for me."

He sat down next to her on the block. "Anything for you, princess."

Addy inhaled deeply. "Before I die, I want you to put me inside a sculpture."

Mack jumped up. "What?"

"I want you to bronze me."

Mack blinked and took a step back. "You mean, like, make molds and do a bronze statue? I can do, but that's a costly commission."

Addy shook her head. "Sorry. I guess I wasn't being clear. I mean me. Dunk me in bronze."

Mack started laughing. Addy stared at him until he stopped. His face, still red from laughing, went sullen.

"I am perfectly serious."

His hands shook and he took a few more steps away from her. "How can you ask me that after we just—I'm not ready for you to die. And I'm not going to help you do it."

She looked at her feet. "I'm going to die no matter what. I'd like to die being part of something bigger than myself." She looked up, demanding that he look her straight in the eye. "I want to be part of the world. I never have been, you know. Not in life."

Mack shook his head, "I can't do it."

Tom's voice called out across the huge warehouse, "Can't do what?"

Neither of them had heard him come in.

Mack swallowed, then said angrily, "Ask the angel of death over here."

Tom looked at her. "What's he talking about?"

Addy shrugged, "It's nothing. Just a stupid fight."

Mack walked over to the sink, turning away from both of them. He gripped the edge so hard it turned his knuckles white.

"You two should go." He turned back to face them with a pointed, hostile glare at Addy. "It's gonna be a while before I'm done, but I have what I need."

There it was. Regret. Addy felt a sob rising. She had to get out of there fast. Silently she pulled on her coat and then ran out the door.

Tom called out behind her, "Addy! Your shoes!" When she didn't turn back, he ran after her.

When he got to the car he asked, "What the hell just happened in there?"

Addy started crying.

Things got worse for her after that. She was confined to her bed for the next week. Surrounded by the things she loved, but filled with her own grief and bombarded by the sorrow of both Tom and her mother.

Each day was a chore for Addy. She kept waiting for death to come, but it stayed away. Mom and Tom's brave faces faded to pale expressions of gloom. It was hard to have a conversation without one of them bursting into tears.

She started to pretend to be asleep whenever they entered the room. The doctor came to see her, tried to urge her to accept treatment, but she adamantly refused. Without treatment, it could be minutes, or it could be a year. What was unspoken was that if it didn't work, it could make her feel worse before dying. Doctors. Addy was sick of them.

The doctor finally prescribed morphine for the pain. Mrs. Clover, fearing that Addy would do the worst, kept it with her in her own room, out of reach.

A week passed. Then two, then three, and still death did not come. Finally, one morning at three a.m., her cell phone rang. It was Mack. He sounded drunk.

"I've just been talking with Tom. He says it's really bad."

Addy's voice was rough and weak. "Yes."

"I didn't tell him what you asked," Mack said.

Addy waited for him to go on. She heard the tinkle of ice cubes in a glass, and Mack swearing under his breath. "I'll do it. What you asked. I understand now."

Tears rolled down Addy's cheeks. Relief. "Thank you."

"Be outside in ten minutes. I'll call you a cab."

Addy struggled to her feet. The only thought that slowed her down was her mother. There was no time to leave a note. A sudden wave of euphoria overcame her. Whether it was the painkiller or the fact that it would all be over soon, she couldn't tell, but it gave her the strength she needed to get out of the house and meet the waiting cab.

Mack's greeting was subdued. It was clear that he was still drunk. He stood back as she entered, and took her coat silently, his expression unreadable.

She looked around the warehouse. The black, makeshift blinds covered all of the windows. Huge white candles, placed all around, provided most of the light. A long rectangular table that hadn't been there on her previous visits was set up in the middle of the room. It was covered by a lace tablecloth, and atop that food, wine, and sheaves of paper.

Without preamble, Mack directed her to the table. The paper contained blueprints of the process her body was about to undergo. Addy suspected that they were designed specifically to scare her into changing her mind.

He explained in annoyingly flat, pedantic detail what he was going to do to her corpse in order to make her wish come true. He included the type of sedative that he planned to slip into her drink. After that, he would smother her with a pillow.

She would be stripped. Then a cast would be made, but unlike other, traditional methods, she would be left inside the cast. He would have to remove her eyes and replace them with marble before dipping her body into the bronze. Addy fought the urge to lift her hands to her face. She would be dead. It didn't matter what he did to her eyes.

She refused to look away from the sketch. Even the tool he would use to perform the eye plucking procedure was rendered in precise detail. Noticing that, she cast a wondering glance at Mack. Had he thought about it this hard because he wanted to fulfill her wish, or was it something else?

She remembered her initial doubts about him, Tom's words, "I heard some things," her mother's immediate dislike. She shook it off. Mack was a different person when it was just herself and Tom. That could not have been a lie.

One of the vats in the far corner began to bubble. Addy swallowed, feeling the heat emanating from that corner of the room.

"Thirsty?" Mack asked, speech over.

He poured wine for them both. Addy watched the purplish red flow from the dusky green bottle into long-stemmed crystal. She stared at the fine gold hairs on the back of Mack's hand as he carefully mixed the powdered narcotic into her glass. This was it. Her first taste of illegal drugs and the prelude to death chosen, rather than predetermined by the failings of her own body. Her mind oscillated between a sense of liberation and one of hesitation.

He raised his own, untainted glass of wine to her. There was no joy in his voice when he said, "Here is to making your beauty and presence immortal."

He drained the glass and poured another, leaving it at the small table. A red circular stain began to form on the delicate white lace tablecloth beneath it.

Addy turned to the bubbling vat of bronze, and another wave of heat washed over her, causing her cheeks to flush. Suddenly, she was filled with rage—at her failing body, at herself for sinking into such despair that this wild idea seemed acceptable. How stupid she felt, giving up just when she was beginning to really experience life. And what about Mack? Had she been wrong? How could he have stayed away for so long, knowing that she was dying?

Tom and her mother's faces flitted across her mind. They would miss her. They would be in pain when she was gone. Why hadn't she considered that? Even if she wasn't willing to fight for herself, shouldn't she be willing to fight for them, the way they had fought with each other for her sake? Why was she willing to give up so easily? It occurred to her that she could wait for Mack's back to turn and push him into the vat, but pragmatism stopped her. The cancer had made her weak; it was impossible to find the strength, and she didn't really want to see him dead.

Mack followed her gaze and, as if her will had exerted itself over the scene, he turned and took a few steps toward the vat.

Without thinking about it, Addy switched her wine glass with his. He turned around to face her and she acted as if she had been reaching for a piece of fudge. She hoped as he picked up the wine, he wouldn't realize that the stain no longer matched up with the base of the glass.

"Addy," he said, concern clouding his face, "are you sure you're ready to do this? You know you can back out if that's what you want."

Her first inclination was to confess. She wasn't feeling brave enough, wasn't ready to die; and her first response to any question was always the honest one. But she still couldn't be certain of his sincerity.

"I'm sure," she said. The hand holding the glass shook.

Suddenly, his facial expression softened. "Well," he said in a hushed tone, "one last kiss, then."

Addy closed her eyes, shaking as he leaned in to her, lightly brushing her lips with his own. The kiss was brief and light, but it lingered like a heavy stain.

Mack backed away, lifted the glass to his mouth, and once again drained it. "You should probably get naked now."

She clutched the lapels of her robe and shook her head. "I'm too shy."

A shadow of disappointment flitted across Mack's countenance. "Modesty is not going to matter in a few minutes."

A few minutes? He hadn't passed out yet. Addy grimaced. "Can't you just do it after I'm asleep?"

Mack lifted the bottle of wine and placed it to his lips once more. "In spite of what you may think of me, necrophilia is not really my thing." He leered at her, waiting, swaying unsteadily. He looked at the wine bottle still in his hand. "Wow. This wine has way more kick to it than I thought."

The bottle slipped out of his hand and shattered as it hit the cement. He blinked, sleepily. "What the—"

Mack crashed down to the floor, following the trajectory of the wine bottle. She walked over to him, careful to avoid the broken glass, and leaned over.

"I'm sorry," she said as his eyes fluttered closed.

Late Night at Marko's

Marko's Swift Mart is located at the intersection of a country road and a stretch of seldom used and poorly maintained highway. Cheryl works the graveyard shift. Marko calls it the dog shift. She often sees two dots like red-glowing eyes across the dark parking lot.

It's a sleepy town so she doesn't worry about late night robbers. The worst fear she ever experienced working behind the counter at Marko's Swift Mart was when a group of stoned high school kids accidentally knocked over an aisle shelf. The source of her terror was Marko's wrath if she didn't get the mess cleaned up. Marko was an easy boss, but he loathed extra work.

Right across the road from Marko's Swift Mart is an empty lot. Gravel, garbage, some old rusty farm equipment and reedy weeds dot the place. Sometimes, cars pull into it. Usually the cars contain teenagers who want to make out, or weary travelers looking for a convenient place to rest their eyes. Red tail lights often show through the glass storefront at night. Darkness brings a shift in depth perception for Cheryl, which is why she does not worry about the red eyes that appear at random.

Cheryl is a college student. Sophomore. Home from school for the summer and filling in Marko's dog shift because it's a family business and he can pay her under the table to cut down on the overhead. Tourists come through in the summer. Not a lot, but enough to make a big difference in profit. Fisherman, hunters, campers, wildlife photographers. Most of the dog shift entails cleaning, restocking shelves, and ringing out munchies for local stoners, drunks, and insomniacs. There is a lot of down time. Cheryl likes to spend that time reading fiction, but sometimes she gets through her books too quickly and starts paging through the magazines on the rack. Once in a while her old friend from high school, Josie, stops by to keep her company.

Josie went to trade school for hairdressing and stays in town, working in her mom's salon. Cheryl feels their high school connection fading already, interests diverging, ways of seeing the world coming into conflict. Tonight, the red eyes are larger; they seem closer even though the pitch black outside the window offers no other object by which to judge distance. Perhaps, thinks Cheryl, it is a newer model of car with bigger tail lights.

The store phone rings. Like everything else inside, it is ancient. Clunky design. Pale yellow receiver and base stained darker in some places from ancient tobacco smoke. Cigarettes are still allowed inside the store in spite of legislation, as long as no customers are present. Cheryl wipes it down every day with antibacterial cleaner, tells Marko he should get a new one, maybe a sleek new portable. Preferably black, to hide the dirt. She picks it up on the third ring.

"Marko's."

"Hey, Cheryl. It's Josie. Drank too much coffee today and can't fall asleep. Feel like some company?"

"Sounds great," says Cheryl. It doesn't actually sound great, but it sounds better than reading through the local paper for the third time. Josie usually has a couple of pieces of good gossip from her clients.

"Cool. Be there in five," Josie's over-bright voice announces.

Cheryl hangs up the phone and goes to the right side of the store to check on the coffee. One pot gives off a charred scent, so she takes it off the burner, dumps it in the hand wash sink beside the coffee makers and then starts another pot. Lacking anything better to do, Cheryl stands next to the machine, impotently wiping at old stains on the so-called stainless steel percolator. She fixes a coffee for herself from the fresh pot and another for Josie, who likes her coffee with a ton of sugar and artificially flavored non-dairy creamers. Cheryl understands sugar. She can get behind that. The use of flavored non-dairy creamers bugs Cheryl, now. At school, there are gourmet coffee shops every few blocks and her friends drink espressos and lattes. Cheryl can now taste the difference between high end coffee and convenience store swill, which makes her own cup of coffee slightly less enjoyable; but she isn't drinking it for the pleasure, she's drinking it for the caffeine.

Cheryl hears Josie's car door slam shut in the convenience store lot and carries their coffees to the front counter to wait. The red eyes in the window wink out and fluorescent overhead lights flicker. It's a creepy coincidence and the hairs on the back of her neck stand up.

She waits a few seconds longer than it should take for Josie to get from the car to the front door. Sipping her coffee, she grimaces as much for the waiting as for the bad taste. Josie is probably re-applying lipstick. She often arrives at the convenience store completely dolled-up, a ready excuse on her lips: "You never know who you'll run into." Cheryl subscribed to the same idea in her high school days, when it sometimes seemed like the only escape from her small town existence was to marry a lonesome traveler of wealth. Now it seemed to her more of an idea that might make someone easy prey to serial killers passing through. She watches a lot of crime drama on television.

A few more seconds pass and Cheryl frowns, wondering if something is wrong. Perhaps the ancient car Josie drives is making some animal noise that she is trying to figure out? Cheryl puts her coffee down on the cracked and yellowing counter and walks to the front door. She peers through the glass, but the space beyond is pitch black; not even the bright store sign casts enough light to see, which is itself unusual. Cheryl raises her hand to the metal door handle. Block letters etched into steel instruct her to push, and she is ready to oblige, except that the lights begin to flicker again. The effect is dramatic this time, disorienting. Her hand rests on the handle as she looks up. The light's strobe irritates and she turns back toward the glass door.

Two red eyes, clear almond shapes, stare back at her from just behind the glass, floating just under the top of the window frame. Cheryl feels the muscles in her throat tighten as one red eye shrinks to a sliver, an eyelid-shaped curtain of darkness hiding its fierce, flaming color.

A flash like lightning leaps from the metal doorframe to her hand and she falls backward into a rack of beef jerky. A multitude of sounds blend together to make one; whispers, wind, the beating of wings, and, distantly, a scream. She feels the edges of plastic packaging digging into her back; the scratches on her arms from the metal spokes of the jerky rack are cold, burning. She sees everything through a red haze and struggles to rise.

When she manages it, the surface beneath her feet feels like sponge. Cheryl imagines herself being absorbed by her environment even as she moves through it. She is liquid that merges with the floor, the sound, the door. When she reaches the door, she moves through it and reaches the dark parking lot whole, herself.

Red eyes perform a slow blink and Cheryl cannot help looking into their depths. Like clear stone, there are no facets but a sense of texture, distortion. Visions lie within and whispers grow both louder and less distinct. Cheryl is submerged. Images of far-flung places zoom past; it is like going through a tunnel at high speeds, glimpsing scenes through a small round window. Stars explode. Castles crumble. Strange creatures swim through gas clouds and beds of algae. Faces emerge and recede too quickly to identify, features blur. Cheryl feels pressure between her eyes, at the top of her nose. The red eyes in the parking lot move away from her, and the visions stop. She lurches forward, stops herself against the trunk of Josie's car.

The red gaze that so hypnotized her is not gone, but turned elsewhere, toward Josie. The driver's side door is open, one of Josie's legs is outside of the car. She is wearing leggings and high-heeled boots. Cheryl can see a corner of a long faux leather jacket, and Josie's pale hand twitches against her thigh. The nails are blood red, and colorful plastic rings glitter in the light shed by Marko's sign, which flickers.

Cheryl feels numb. She sees the outline of the creature that belongs to the red gaze.

It is seven feet tall, at least, and looks vaguely like a man. Soft, furry antennae protrude from its head, like a gypsy moth. Wings hang from its back and fan out like a cape; they blur with movement and shed dust on Josie's car, her leg. *She won't like that when she wakes up*, Cheryl thinks.

Josie's hand stops moving and the creature crouches beside the car. Its antennae twitch and it takes flight. Because it is dark, Cheryl cannot see where it goes, but is aware of its movement. Trees to the north. She knows that the creature will not turn its face toward her again.

Now that it is gone, shock fades and fear comes. Her voice shakes as she calls out, "Josie?"

Cheryl half runs, half stumbles to the open car door, touches her friend's hand. The skin is cold. Josie stares blankly at Cheryl. Her mascara lies in streaks down her face. Cheryl can see little grains of mascara mixing with Josie's tears like silt. She blinks and the detail goes away.

Cheryl blinks again and suddenly she knows that if Josie leaves Marko's at 3:30 a.m. she will land in a car accident and lose a hand, but if she leaves at 2:45 a.m. she will arrive at home, and life will continue unchanged. Now it is Cheryl's hand that twitches. Josie makes a high-pitched noise as she exhales, like air leaking out of a tire.

Cheryl whispers, "Josie?"

The word feels forced and like it is coming from somewhere far away, outside her own throat. It is then that she notices a low hum in her ears.

Josie mutters under her breath and Cheryl thinks she hears a string of names, recognizing Josie's ex-boyfriends. Josie's eyelids flutter and Cheryl wonders if her high school friend will know something, too. Cheryl leans down to touch Josie's cheek. "Wake up."

Josie's eyes flutter open. This close, Cheryl can see herself reflected in Josie's pupils and what she sees there causes her to back away from her friend. Josie screams. Other reflective surfaces offer confirmation.

Cheryl's eyes glow red like tail lights in the dark.

Ewe Bluhdprat and the All-Knowing Gargoyle

Ewe Bluhdprat shivers like a dead jellyfish getting poked with a stick. He shivers and waits, but cannot tell if he shivers because he is nervous or because it is cold.

He waits beside the huge, all-knowing gargoyle which guards the front steps of the entrance to Mastiff Public Library. The gargoyle isn't actually omniscient. Ewe has just always thought of it as such because when he was a child, his mother used to call it the all-knowing gargoyle. It is an object that makes him feel protected, safe.

Ewe blows on his hands through his knit mittens. The only gloves he owns are mittens, which are good for snowball fights and a kind of sticky warmth. As his fingers rub together inside the mittens, Ewe's hands sweat. Mittens are not good for lighting cigarettes, text-messaging or pulling triggers. Ewe knows the last item on the list is true because he tried it at the shooting range during target practice last week.

A minute goes by—then five—and soon Ewe is not sure how long he has been standing in the snow beside the all-knowing gargoyle. The gargoyle casts its far-reaching shadow across the white library lawn. It makes Ewe think of people who are able to tell what time of day it is by the direction shadows fall. He is not one of them and doubts that he would have the patience to learn.

When he was a boy, Ewe used to whisper all of his secrets into the gargoyle's ear. Secret crushes and his meanest thoughts. The gargoyle might have been menacing, but it never changed expression. It did not judge.

Ewe shivers again, still waiting. He shivers even when it is not cold. He is a jittery man, and painfully aware of the characteristic. This, he blames on his name, though not on the parents who named him. They were kind and loving, maybe a bit short-sighted. In grade school, whenever someone called out something like, "You jerk!" Ewe always thought the person doing the shouting was speaking to him. Every song about hearts breaking or hearts soaring or hearts bleeding felt as if they were being directed to him, too. The song issue was much easier to cope with as it was impossible that any of the honey-voiced singers knew anything about him, and in any case he never dated until college.

He never could find a way to shake the other problem. Even at this moment, while he shivers and waits next to the all-knowing gargoyle, he worries that a passing stranger will address someone who is not Ewe as you, and unknowingly add to his anxiety. This constant worry over misunderstandings regarding his name was often overwhelming to Ewe.

He wonders if he should, this one last time, confess to the all-knowing gargoyle. He looks into its face but its cold dead concrete eyes tell him that today he cannot afford to be sentimental.

A bus stops in front of the library. A woman who carries a sullen toddler on her hip struggles to descend the bus's steps with a folded stroller. The toddler's left hand is covered by a blue mitten, the mitten's twin dangles precariously from a worn-looking thread. Ewe catches his breath and holds it, thinking that the dangling mitten will snag on something and be lost to its brother forever. "No, not the mitten," he mutters.

He cannot take the anticipation. Ewe exhales and rushes forward to help the woman with the stroller. In a second she is off the bus, smiling. Before she can say, "Thank you," Ewe points to the library entrance and says, "Going in there?"

The woman blinks, hugs her child to herself a bit tighter and says, "Yes," which sounds more like a question than a statement. Ewe knows what she is thinking. She worries that this strange man might be a threat to her child and by extension herself and the rest of her family. Ewe does not mind. In fact, he is flattered and thinks, "I could get used to being a man who is feared." More often in real life, which does not include moments like this, Ewe Bluhdprat is ridiculed.

He picks up the stroller and turns away from the frightened woman and her child, hiding his inappropriate grin. He takes the library steps two at a time, careful to carry the stroller high enough so that it does not bang against the stairs as he ascends. He leaves the stroller at the door and trots back down the steps to his spot next to the gargoyle. His grin is gone. The woman seems to have lost her fear.

As the woman walks up the library steps, child squirming on her hip, she calls out, "Thank you!"

Ewe winces but clenches his teeth into something like a smile and answers, "You're welcome."

He waits for the glass door to fall shut behind her, shivers when it does, and reaches a mittened hand into his pocket. He touches an object that is hard metal and reassuring. This object is an old friend, and right now it is his only friend. Perhaps it is his one true love.

The person Ewe thought was his one true love left him for his ex-boss. She never told him why, but he knows why. Ewe is twitchy; his ex-boss is not. His ex-boss is an exemplary suit. This other man is a calm and steady—if self-important—person with gleaming hair plugs and an unfettered smile. The other man loves himself with zero doubts, Ewe feels the opposite which is something he knows is hard for another person to deal with, sometimes. Ewe tries not to think about his ex-wife, which frees him up to focus all of his anger and frustration on the man who stole his life.

"Ewe, you make our clients uncomfortable and that is just not an appropriate quality in an employee at a public relations firm," said the ex-boss on what Ewe now thinks of as D-day. When he returned home that same afternoon carrying a small cardboard box containing his personal items from his cubicle, the wife was already packed and gone. A note was taped to the aluminum foil covering a tray of lasagna.

All it said was, "I'm sorry. Goodbye and good luck."

Ewe could not bring himself to eat the lasagna and went out that night for fast food. Passing the window of an upscale restaurant, he had seen his newly ex-wife eating and laughing with his newly ex-boss. Ducking around the corner before they spotted him, he felt rage well up and spill over. The intense emotion was vaguely liberating. Ewe had experienced rage, but it had always been directed inwardly, at the self. This time, he had an outward target. He wasn't sure what to do with it.

That night was the first since grade school that Ewe had resorted to talking to the all-knowing gargoyle. That night, he repeatedly asked the gargoyle, "Why?" and offered it a swallow of whiskey from a brown paper bag. The all-knowing gargoyle stared blankly, unable to offer any comfort other than the fact of its fixed position. It could not flee Ewe Bluhdprat's company.

Waiting, today, in front of the Mastiff Public Library, Ewe shivers as he waits for the ex-boss to show up. Ostensibly, the point of this meeting is for Ewe to recover a few books and CDs that went missing when she left.

The clicking of purposeful and well-heeled shoes sounds against the frigid pavement. "This is it," Ewe whispers to the gargoyle.

Ewe shivers, pulls off his mittens, takes the gun out of his pocket, and waits. *Click, click, click,* shout the shoes. *Now, now, now,* hollers Ewe's over-eager heart. He shivers and cannot wait.

Ewe steps out of the long shadow of the all-knowing gargoyle, takes aim at the approaching man's heart, and fires. The man makes eye contact with Ewe, his expression one of confusion as he topples. It takes less than a second for Ewe's emotions to mirror that of the fallen man. It takes one and a half seconds for Ewe's plan of violent retribution to twist in on itself, for the target to shift.

Ewe falls back into the gargoyle's shadow, trains the gun on his own head and pulls the trigger. Brain matter splatters the gargoyle's head.

The Arrival of Sadie Cullen Carlyle

Madison Carlyle sat on the front steps of her mother June's red brick two-family colonial absently massaging her ankles. No rain, yet. The gray sky could thunder down upon Brickman's Run any second, or it might just be teasing. Madison's mother, June, was in the backyard, rearranging her multiple lawn ornaments, bird feeders, and faux marble statues. Madison hated those things. The pink flamingos and bright, oversized butterflies did not go with the cheap, hollow replicas of the Venus de Milo and Michelangelo's David.

The garden itself was overgrown with ivy, already insinuating its destructive power over the high wood fence, which had long ago begun to splinter. The slats which had long ago been painted like crayons were now marred by gaps, and their colors were fading unevenly. A bright red crayon showed streaks of puce, the green had deadened to a grayish amalgam. June claimed to spend a little time each day pulling weeds, but Madison never saw any sign of their diminishment.

Madison frowned at the gray day, the fact that she'd had to move home, and the thought of her mother, June, shuffling lazily about the garden in her housedress and curlers. To be fair, Madison knew that if a gauche garden was all she really had to complain of, she was pretty lucky. Other mothers of women her age were much worse. The situation was her fault. If she hadn't gotten pregnant, she'd still be independent. She shifted her weight, settling on the steps.

The second family was a group of college students who rented from June. Officially, there were three students on the lease; but it was difficult to tell how many of the kids were residents, and how many used the place as a crash pad. June had promised the rented half of the home to Madison after the baby came. The students would be gone in three months, but she couldn't help worrying about the damage they might be inflicting on the space. Every time the front door opened, beer and other suspicious scents wafted toward her. The trash on the rental side of the front yard was hard to ignore. Cigarette butts littered the lawn and choked the grass just like June's ivy asphyxiated the backyard fence.

The students were also in the habit of feeding neighborhood cats. Most of the cats had owners, so they didn't linger. The housecats came to check out the chaos of their yard and play with their feline friends. The strays were a different story. They lingered, yowling, scratching, biting; distributing feces and fur-balls like candy. June had a hard time keeping up with the spillover, but would not allow Madison to help clean up.

Madison wondered where all the strays were coming from. Brickman's Run was a tiny community on the outskirts of Dead River, laid out on a grid about ten blocks deep and wide. It boasted a single gas station and convenience store where you could purchase hot dogs, slush drinks, and fish bait. The college was an easy twenty-minute drive, except during the winter months. There were not a lot of places the cats could come from. Most of Madison and June's neighbors were dog owners.

Most of the cats ignored humans, using the lazy generosity of the students in a purely opportunistic way. One cat, however, disdained the others of his species, which perhaps explained his lack of fleas. Madison thought he must have a home nearby. His tuxedo coat was a deep, shiny black, the white paws and chest patch were clean. He also seemed disinterested in the students' offerings of tuna and cheap wet cat food. Instead, he visited sporadically, and then only to warm himself on the brick stairway up to

Madison and June's front door. Occasionally he sat at Madison's feet, blinking his green eyes and purring.

One other significant difference separated him from the other strays; he was polydactyl, which gave him the appearance of having an opposable thumb. Madison had read about these kinds of cats. They were supposed to be lucky. She called him Cullen, after a boy she'd had a crush on in grade school.

Cullen the human died with his mother and father in a car crash when he was thirteen. He'd been on his way to school when an ambulance blew through a stop sign at a four-way intersection. It was a rural road, but the tall foliage at the edges of the road had not been cut. There was no view in any direction because of the unfettered greenery. Cullen had been on his way to school.

Later, Madison found out that he died with a note written in black ink on a piece of loose leaf that had been folded into a triangle. It had been written to her. Cullen was going to ask her to the school dance.

Madison liked to think that the cat was a manifestation of the first Cullen. She would never admit to anyone out loud that she sometimes believed that if Cullen had lived to take her to that first dance, her love life would have been less tragic. Her thirteen-year-old self had been convinced that he was her forever lover, though their lips had never touched.

Overhead, the clouds darkened, underscoring the threat of rain. Madison thought that perhaps Cullen the cat would not come to pay her a visit on the stairs.

She heard the back door slam shut, and knew that her mother had abandoned the out-of-control garden. Next door, the cats on the lawn meowed and scattered for cover. Madison waited, unwilling to budge until the very first drops of rain fell.

A thunderclap sounded, and Cullen the cat appeared at the bottom of the steps.

Madison gave him a closed-lip smile. "Where did you come from?"

Cullen blinked at her and ambled up the stairs. He rubbed his head against her ankles, purring, and jumped into her lap for the first time.

Madison felt a shiver of pleasure travel the length of her spine as the cat settled by kneading her knees with his mitten-like forepaws. She stroked his glossy black fur, and he purred so intensely that the sound blended with the low, rumbling thunder that rolled toward Brickman's Run.

Inside, June banged around the kitchen. "Madison," she called. "Are you coming in for lunch?"

"In a minute, Mom," Madison called back. She sighed and scratched the top of Cullen's head. "I wish I could take you inside with me."

Cullen's ears twitched, but he gave no other sign that her words registered. Madison suspected that Cullen had no interest in a life confined by walls, doors, windows and locks. Minutes passed and the rain politely refused to come, although the rumbles of thunder increased.

June's bare feet padded across the hardwood floor of the foyer. She called to Madison through the screen door. "Honey, lunch is ready."

Madison turned, without rising, to face her mother. "Okay."

June noticed Cullen the cat on Madison's lap. Her lips pulled into a grim line of disapproval. "You're never supposed to let a cat sit on your lap when you're pregnant. You leave him alone and come in here, right now."

Cullen meowed, jumped off Madison's lap, and ran off. She watched him turn around a corner.

As soon as he was out of view, she felt the first juicy raindrop hit the center of her forehead. She shivered as more warning droplets fell from the sky and chased her inside.

The interior of June and Madison's home was more organized than the garden, though it still showed signs of clutter. Unfinished books open face down on the coffee table showed dust in the cracks of their stressed spines. Mismatched throw pillows intended for the couch lay strewn in different locations; one under the coffee table, another on the bench of the out-of-tune piano, and yet another sat in a wicker basket with junk mail and old catalogs.

Still, it was comfortable. It was home.

Madison made her way through the living room to the kitchen at the back of the house. The walls were painted a soothing pale green and the room itself was full of light. Faux sunflowers in various configurations decorated and brightened the space, though the grayness of the day dampened the light, airy feel. Madison sat on a wooden chair opposite June at the high, round table. Cucumber sandwiches, cold blueberry tea, and seasoned French fries were presented appealingly.

June's expression remained grim, even as Madison offered a warm smile and thanked her for preparing a lovely lunch. "You should not have let that cat sit on your lap."

Madison's smile faltered. "Mom, what are you talking about?"

"If a cat sits on your lap when you're pregnant, your baby will be born with its face."

Madison laughed, "That's ridiculous, Mom."

June shrugged. "Fine. Make fun. But don't say I didn't warn you."

A small television sat on the counter within easy view of the table, so June turned it on and increased the volume using the ever-present remote control. Madison was grateful for its presence; the television set saved her suffering uncomfortable silences during most meals shared with June.

The rain came in loud torrents, turning the large kitchen window that looked out onto the garden into a waterfall, transforming the scene beyond it into a blur of muted colors. Thunder rolled and Madison felt a turning in her belly.

"Hush, now," she whispered to her restless fetus.

***

Three months passed with no sign of Cullen the Cat; it was as if the thunderstorm had borne him away. Madison asked at the Brickman's Run convenience store if anyone had seen or owned a cat fitting Cullen's description, but no one knew what she was talking about.

"Besides," a clerk with graying hair and kind, matronly eyes said, "I hear that cats aren't all that great to have around newborns."

Disappointed, Madison gave up looking for Cullen. The pace of life sped up. The baby's first day of greeting the world outside Madison's womb approached and the house needed to be prepared.

Damage to the property was not as bad as Madison suspected. Most of it was cosmetic. There were holes to be patched, rooms to be painted, floors that had to be cleaned and waxed, and junk to be removed. The worst of it was the mess in the yard. June had been smart not to put in carpet. Since Madison was pregnant, June would not allow her to help with painting, so she was on trash duty. A need for frequent breaks made the days feel long, the work more burdensome. Madison felt annoyed that she couldn't just plow through her tasks as she would have before her tummy blew up like a basketball.

Carrying a large, sturdy trash bag in one hand, Madison squatted to pick up trash from the yard and felt a brief pang in her abdomen. She winced, and paused mid-reach to take a deep breath. The pain subsided, so she continued gathering garbage; fast food wrappers, a coffee can that had been used as an ashtray, and several empty aluminum cans. They had once contained beer.

Having cleared a small area, Madison shuffled over a few inches to clear more debris. More cans. Another twitch of pain, and the feeling of muscles contracting of their own accord. She called for June and bore down, noticing as she clenched that one of the cans was marked Cullen's, a hard to find brand of beer that wasn't very good. She closed her eyes and smiled at the instant connection of can to cat to childhood love, and then gave herself over to the demands of her body. The baby was coming. Madison must live, now, in the physical tidal exchange of euphoria and pain.

Sadie Cullen Carlyle arrived with a mewling cry and a gurgle amid throw pillows and blankets on June's fading floral couch. Though not premature, she was unusually small, with a face and head covered in fur. Two pointed ears topped either side of her skull, her mouth was unusually wide, her jaw pointed, and a mild harelip split her upper lip so cleanly in the center that it did not interfere with her nose, nor expose teeth.

Madison could not afford the expensive surgeries that might give Sadie a more human appearance. Grandmother

June tried hard not to say, "I told you so." Madison however would not have heard, for she was entranced by her daughter's exotic beauty, and loved the way she purred whenever she lay in Madison's lap.

Fork You - A Gladiola Johnson Story (For Proserpine)

She was wet. Covered in mud. Crunchy dead leaves and bugs stuck to her hair, her tattered blue dress. A filmy stickiness covered her teeth, like slug slime over rocks - the result of dehydration and a lack of toothpaste. As she walked, she clinked; a belt made of frayed twine hung loosely about her straight, childhood waist, dangling a wood-carved fork and spoon. The little girl had no idea of the mechanical, linear passage of time, she had no point of reference to divide the days and months spent amid the browns and greens of the woods near the Johnson sprawl. The speechless creatures that lived there could not have told her the date and she shared their sense of things.

The sunlight that hit her face when she emerged from the trees into a field of high yellow grass was blinding, but it felt good, clean. She'd been drawn to the place by unfamiliar noises, human voices, music, laughter. Sounds alien to her.

Hidden by the tall grass, she waited in a crouch, expectant and alert. Her heart beat as fast as a bird's. She heard rustling, footfalls, and saw subtle movements in the grass. The motion whispered a warning of something approaching. As it was about to pass by, she grabbed its foot. Her hands were lightning quick, detaching a fork from the belt of twine as her prey fell forward. Instinctively, her arm lunged as she attempted to stick the fork in the creature's leg, but it was faster than she was, and much larger.

It bellowed and moaned. "Damn, girl! What are you trying to do?"

The girl snarled at the big two-legged beast that was all at once so similar to herself and so different, so much larger and louder. She'd seen one like him before. She jabbed with her fork and missed.

The beast threw its head back and laughed, which sounded to the girl like strange barking. She sat down and whimpered defeat.

The giant stopped barking and looked at her quietly. "I don't recognize you, child."

The girl stared mutely at him.

"You look like you're expectin' to get ate up."

She stood and backed away.

"Don't you talk?"

The girl cocked her head to the side, like a dog trying to figure out if someone is friend or foe.

"I'll take that as a no."

Girl and man stared at each other for a few moments, each waiting for the other to move first. The girl clutched her fork close to her chest and the skies above darkened. The rain came fast, hard and heavy. She closed her eyes and lifted her face to the rain. Water pulled the dirt away in muddy streaks. The man scooped her up and carried her, screaming, across the field, toward shelter, toward a cage.

***

The Johnson family was a huge brood with a knotted family tree. They lived on a heavily wooded plot of thirty acres, which was itself surrounded by more densely wooded, unpopulated plots. Beyond the wooded areas lay abandoned strip mines, barren tracts of land along rarely traveled single-lane highways dotted with heaps of slag and colorful patches of vegetation. Housing on the Johnson land consisted of randomly situated trailers, haphazardly built shacks and pavilions. Rumors of horrific living conditions that abounded in the municipality of Varksnort Haven were, in some cases, truthful. There was a local ordinance stating that if an ambulance was called on to the Johnson property, they were not to respond, the exposure to unhygienic conditions there deemed too risky to the health of the local populace.

Legend had it that the twelve Johnson brothers enjoyed the custom of wife swapping with such enthusiasm and voraciousness that the thirty Johnson children did not know who their fathers really were, but shared many uncles. This also was true, but only to a point. Not all of the youngsters on the Johnson property were actually Johnsons. Some of the kids were friends of other Johnson kids who, before becoming assimilated into the infamous clan, had suffered even worse home lives, kicked out by wrathful parents, neglected by abusive ones, or simply forgotten. The Johnsons' cleanliness and sexual morals might have been questionable, but no one could say that they never showed kindness to strays.

The wild child that had come to them had definitely found the right place, even if they did have to keep her in a dog cage until she could behave well enough to run with their rough-and-tumble pack. The Johnson that found her was named Jed. Tall, affable, and furry, he was always clad in a red flannel shirt with the sleeves cut off, no matter the weather. He was fond of flexing his biceps and saying, "It's one of them there imperatives to show off guns like these." His smile was the biggest in the county, largely due to the fact that after decades of recycled Johnson genes, Jed had twelve extra teeth. "One for each brother," as the clan liked to say. Luckily for Jed, his mouth was large enough to accommodate the extra tools of mastication, so that they never caused him discomfort.

The girl, unlike the excess teeth, did cause Jed Johnson pain. Because he had been the one to find her, the family voted that he would be the one she could call "Daddy," a unique and freakish title to hold on the Johnson sprawl. Though Jed was still tender at the age of 29, the title made him feel old, and Gladiola made him feel even older. She kicked and snarled, she stole food, refused to speak, or even learn to speak. She pulled hair, bit into throats and hamstrings indiscriminately, and brandished her wooden utensils as weapons. This was not necessarily out of line with Johnson behavior, but it was only tolerated toward outsiders. The Johnsons frowned upon turning on one's own. This crazy girl was literally ready to bite every hand that tried to feed her.

So Jed Johnson unearthed a big, sturdy dog cage to put her in. Strangely enough, she seemed to like it. As soon as she was wrangled into the cage, she started caressing the cool, smooth metal bars and quieted down. What sent the girl into a mad, rabid fit of rage was the confiscation of her belt. Jed had intended to place the wooden utensils in the general Johnson circulation of Useful Items but changed his mind. To his thinking, the fork and spoon must have been like a security blanket—a connection to the safe and civilized world she'd been in before getting stranded in the woods—and they'd likely also somehow helped her to survive. They were stained a deep reddish brown, as if by blood, which gave Jed the heebie jeebies; but out of kindness, he placed them in a special box and kept them under his bunk until such a time came when the beastly little girl could learn to speak.

Of course, before she could learn to speak, she had to have a name. The idea made Jed nervous. Everything about the girl made him nervous—she had an unshakable meanness in her that he did not wish to name. His brothers wouldn't let him forget about it, and Jed couldn't avoid them. He shared a home with brother George and his sister Martha, which was fairly representative of the other dwellings on the Johnson property. The "house" was an old trailer with a shack built onto the side of it, and a proper garage extended from the shack. The garage was where they kept the caged little girl.

They talked about her while gathered at the round plastic patio table in the kitchen.

"She needs a name," Brother George said, scratching his round, protruding belly.

"Well, you name her then," said Jed.

"No way," George shook his head. "You found her, you name her. You could always at least call her Mutt."

"Don't we got a dog named Mutt?" Jed asked, stalling.

"Well, what about where she came from? Use that," George persisted.

"Nobody knows where she came from. Jes' sprung up outta the ground like a goddamned weed, or flower."

"Name her that then. After some kinda flower."

Jed wrinkled his nose, "I get hay fever. I hate flowers."

George sighed and sat back in his chair, hooking his thumbs into his suspenders. "You don't got any better ideas."

Jed fell silent. His eyes wandered around the kitchen and fell on an old calendar featuring different flowers. It was open to the month of May, with a fading picture of gladiolas in bloom.

"Alright then. Gladiola. Now leave me alone. I gotta get that girl to talk."

George clapped him on the back and congratulated him on his right fine choice. Later, as Jed was being lulled to sleep by the distant howls of that delicate flower, Gladiola Johnson, he smiled to himself, thinking of the new nameplate he would make for her cage.

When Jed next brought Gladiola her meal, he brought it on a battered pewter dish that could have been in use since the days of the Puritans on Plymouth Rock. The meal was equally mundane, to be eaten with the aid of a dull and bent tablespoon. Beef and onions. Oil and rice. Accompanied by a tin cup of well water. The first thing little Gladiola did was bang the spoon against the floor of her cage. Gladiola made a disappointed grunt, brow furrowed in consternation. The single bare light bulb which lit the garage dimmed at random intervals. The changing shadows made little Gladiola's face look demonic.

Jed, who was sitting outside the cage with his own bland meal, beaten plate and abused silverware, thought that the spoon-banging was cute. He smiled.

"Gladiola, that's not how you use a spoon."

She grunted again in response, eyeing him warily. She sat down, clutching her spoon with one hand and sticking a stubby little finger in the mush of meat and starch, then sniffed the finger.

"Gladiola, watch," Jed said, lifting a heaping spoonful of goo to his mouth. His prodigious teeth made fast work of the morsel. He swallowed and patted his belly. "Mmmm. Yummy."

Gladiola sighed like a stubborn old man. Jed tried not to laugh as she wrestled with the spoon. It took her several tries to successfully transfer food to spoon, then to her own mouth. She ended up with half the meal on her already filthy dress. She did manage to eat enough of it though, and the horse tranquilizer Jed had dosed the food with soon took effect.

Though the Johnsons had no horses, they always had horse tranquilizers on hand, in case of emergency. If an outsider noticed and pressed the issue, the Johnsons might have said that it had something to do with bears. However, if an adult outsider stumbled uninvited onto the sprawl, they weren't likely to remember much of the visit, finding themselves by the side of the road feeling groggy and confused. Hypothetically.

It had pained Jed to dose Gladiola, but his sister Martha (or cousin, he wasn't sure which) had insisted that the wild child be groomed. Nobody wanted to receive any more scratches or bruises for the trouble. Once she was safely asleep, he took her from the cage and carried her into the shack where a huge tub of hot water waited.

"My lord, this child has been through a lot," said Martha.

Jed glanced over at Gladiola's back as Martha's overlarge and capable hands scrubbed it. Her skin had a sickly greenish cast to it, like old bruises just beginning to recover, and there were welts, scratches and fresher purple bruises dotting her spine. He swallowed and looked away, disturbed and heartsick. "If that child stays mean it won't be no surprise."

Martha drained the tub and refilled it to rinse the girl off, then wrapped her up in some towels and a baby blue blanket. The towels and blanket were ratty and worn, but clean. The next task was to cut her hair. It was cropped to a page-boy cut, being too tangled to save. It revealed a claw mark behind her left ear.

"Jesus," Jed whispered as he cradled her head. She didn't seem so wild and mean now, clean and sleeping. The nine-year old looked almost sweet.

***

Gladiola's dreams weren't dreams as much as they were hazy recollections colored by the surrealism found only in the subconscious. They were filled with vivid greens and browns, fading to yellows and grays. Trees which sometimes seemed to move with her, human faces etched into the rough lines of bark. Itchiness, threatening animals, losing sandals in a stream. Friendlier animals, nuts and berries, a growling stomach. Cold white of winter light barely filtered through tree branches turned black by damp. Mud caked boots with someone in them, next to her own bare bluish feet. Wrapping her feet in animal skins to make the blue go away. Fire. The bugs scattering on the inside of a hollowed tree where she hid. Hunting rabbits. Catching fish. The taste of chipmunk flesh. The crunch of bones. Running from a mountain lion. The sting of claws to the side of her head. Warm sticky blood. A strange man in a red cloak scaring the mountain lion away, stopping the flow of her blood with the massive frilly cuffs of a white shirt and a few words. The stains she left on the cloth. Being entranced by the man's mouth, full lips, the melodious sound of his voice echoing in her poor brain. The world vibrated when he spoke. She didn't know what it meant when he said, "If I scratch your fuzzy back, little girl, then one day, you shall have to scratch mine." And he had made her something. A belt of twine. The wooden utensils. He showed her how to use them. She understood him when he spoke, but she didn't know how or why. She felt worried that she would not see him again, now that she was with these strange large people. Somehow, she knew the Magic Man wouldn't like them, but his voice came to her again like a blessing. "Don't worry, little one. You have something of mine. You'll see me again." He paused, and smiled. "I have another gift for you, little one. Speech."

And when Gladiola Johnson woke after twelve uninterrupted hours of sleep, she could talk.

Her first words were, "Jed Johnson. you turd! Let me outta this cage!"

Jed's mouth fell open to a wide oblong shape. He blinked, rubbed his eyes and then ran back into the kitchen, where Martha and George were cooking.

"Shit howdy!" said Jed. "She's talking!"

Martha smiled, revealing the gummy gap where her two front teeth used to be before her career as a stripper. Martha was convinced that Gladiola's newfound locutions were due to the magic of the bath. "Ain't nothin' a little soap and water won't fix."

Jed rolled his eyes and ran back out to the garage, and Gladiola.

"When did you learn to talk?"

"Just now, you big lug. Now let me outta here!"

Jed might have had some sympathy for Gladiola, and from the way she stood, ready for a fight, he knew she was as good as any blue-blooded Johnson. Even so, there were limits.

"Now you listen to me, Gladiola Johnson, you can't come outta there until you make me a few promises."

Gladiola growled.

"You gonna listen?"

Gladiola begrudgingly nodded.

"No more bitin', kickin', or scratchin' any of us Johnsons. You can be as mean and nasty as you want to other folk. Most of 'em deserve it, I'll grant you, but us, we're your family now. And you gotta play nice, or at least less mean, with family. Think you can do that?"

Gladiola pouted. Jed stared her down.

"If I say yes, you'll let me out?"

"If you say yes, will you mean it?"

"How would you know if I mean it or not?" asked Gladiola.

Jed shrugged. "Don't matter if I know. I'm bigger than you and so are a lot of the other Johnsons, including ones your own age. We can chuck you back in that cage so fast you won't even know what happened."

"Fine! Now let me out!"

"Okay."

Gladiola was so happy to be let out of the cage that she neglected to ask about her belt. The Magic Man would be angry if it got lost or ruined. And she wanted to play with the magic silverware again. But first, she had some running around to do.

Gladiola ran out to the middle of the field, which was surrounded by a wide horseshoe of old rickety mobile homes. There was only one proper house on the property and it was old, falling into ruin. Patches on the third story roof were covered in duct tape and torn garbage bags. The wrap-around porch sagged and lacked any stairs to climb up. Weeds and ivy overran the place. Fat carpenter bees swarmed, and great piles of wood dust could be seen on what was left of the porch. It was clear that no one lived there anymore.

After she climbed up onto the front porch and fell through the weakened wood, Gladiola stayed away from it and opted to spend the rest of the day running around in the field at the center of the houses. She sometimes stopped to gaze at the tree line, admiring one particularly large tree.

Around the large tree a few smaller trees were clustered. They looked vaguely human in shape, and every once in a while, out of the corner of her eye, Gladiola saw them move. She played a game where she would face the opposite direction of the tree line and wait for a few minutes, then turn around as quickly as she could to see if she could catch them in the act, instead of the wispy impressions she got from witnessing the movement using only peripheral vision. It didn't work, but one or two appeared to have moved away from the tree line toward the edge of the field.

After a full day of blissful freedom, Gladiola found herself exhausted, but without a bed. The Johnsons didn't have an extra one. In fact, the Johnsons didn't have any real beds at all after the lice and bed bug plague that hit the property in 1923. They mostly slept on cots or sturdy wooden bunks piled thick with pillows and blankets, soft items that could easily be removed and washed. It was that very same hygiene scandal which had put the ordinance on the books preventing health care officials from setting foot on the property, and caused the municipality to pay for the property's yearly insecticide needs, regardless of the countless toxins which—along with the shallow Johnson gene pool—may have contributed to Jed's extra teeth. So Gladiola was left with her dog cage, her nest of pillows and blankets, and a groaning space heater that leaned to the left.

Gladiola was a nasty little girl, but she was not by any means a stupid little girl; so she knew that to avoid getting locked in while she slept, she had to remove the door to the dog cage and hide it somewhere. At her insistence, Jed removed the door; but of course, being nine years old, she underestimated her new peers in the Johnson clan.

One of the more endearing Johnson family traits was their inventiveness with tortures and pranks. In fact, some of the family members said to have disappeared had actually been inducted into such organizations as would find the inherited penchant for torture useful—the mafia, the CIA, Hell's Angels, the Vatican... If conspiracy theorists had been able to get their ink-stained hands on this information they would have had a field day. But even the Johnsons didn't know about it, so to this day the secret remains hidden—as hidden as Gladiola's slumber was perilous.

As if Jed had started a new Johnson tradition, the young boys continued to drug Gladiola's dinners with horse tranquilizers so that when she fell asleep at night, they could relocate the dog cage, with Gladiola still inside.

Once the cage was moved, they'd stake out the location in shifts, hoping to catch her waking up in the middle of the night, confused and angry. What the Johnson boys enjoyed most about this pastime was Gladiola's amazing capacity for colorful profanity. Her most excellent swearing was firstly an opportunity for them to be amused, and secondly, to learn new phrases which they used to make them more popular with the other roughnecks in town.

One night, the Johnson boys moved Gladiola's cage to the middle of the field. It was raining, softly, with a heavier storm on the way. They were mischievous boys, but not completely heartless, so they covered the cage with a blue plastic tarp.

Snug inside the cage, under the tarp, Gladiola snored as the air inside grew staler and hotter with each rumble of her deviated septum. There might not have been enough holes in the tarp to let in fresh air, but there were enough to allow moisture to collect inside, making her skin grow sticky. She tossed and turned, twisting her blankets around her body, hair plastered to her sweaty forehead and neck. She dreamed of the Magic Man and his magnificent frilly shirt as he dangled the magic silverware in front of her entranced eyes.

The fork was her favorite. She used it to hunt deer and rabbit. The spoon was less interesting, though useful—the convex side could be applied to any frozen object to thaw it out, or solid things that would liquefy. When she stuck that fork into something alive, it was immediately cooked, and cooked perfectly—the meat sliding easily off the bone, tender and juicy, just the right amount of salt. Gladiola's mouth began to water, making a sticky, uncomfortable mess on her cheek.

It was that puddle of drool which woke her up just in time for the lightning strike on her cage. It melted the plastic tarp, making her blankets burst into flame, and causing the metal cage to grow red with heat. The Johnson boys risked emerging from their hiding place, afraid that they had killed Gladiola, for what man or beast could have escaped such a sudden onslaught of hostility from cruel nature, the capricious cosmos? They didn't need good grades in science to realize little Gladiola was cooked. They howled more fiercely than the winds with grief and guilt over the demise of their new sister.

Gladiola was dazed and dead, or so she thought, as her head buzz-buzzed with damning electricity. She'd been thrown from the cage, shot out in an arc that sent her flying several feet into the high yellow grass. She watched the Johnson boys howling, and grinned. *Serves the bastards right for messing with me,* she thought. *Now I'm a ghost, I'll haunt them.* Hair sticking straight up into the air, clothing reduced to ash-dusted underwear, blue sparks jumping from her fingertips, the wrathful and alive wraith of Gladiola made a beeline for the boys. She waited for their howling to subside to whimpers and tears. She smiled and shouted, "PIGFUCKERS!" at the top of her lungs.

They all jumped. Little JP wet his pants and Gladiola started to laugh. The boys rushed over to her, fighting each other for a hug from Gladiola, calling out to each other and then to her, "She's alive! She's alive! You're alive!"

Gladiola blinked. "I'm alive?"

Just then, Donny threw his arms around her for a hug. There was a zapping sound at the contact, and he jumped back. "Ouch!"

"I'm alive." Gladiola said again. Her smile grew wider. "Even better. You guys owe me."

"We'll do anything, Gladiola! Just don't tell Jed."

She rubbed her sparky hands together, eyes gleaming with lightning and an idea. "You are gonna build me a treehouse to live in."

The boys looked at each other sullenly and agreed wordlessly that they had no choice, but also that the impending physical labor sucked donkey balls.

Gladiola didn't waste any time putting the offending pseudo-siblings to work. As soon as the sun rose, she was barking orders and working on the schematics. (Though her childish renderings proved that both her artistic and architectural reach far exceeded her grasp, they did show a surprising understanding of construction.)

The tree Gladiola chose as her lofty abode was ancient, twisted and gnarled. It was the large tree she had noticed that first day she'd been let out of her cage. It had strong wide branches and blood-red bark—a species of tree as yet unidentified, an arborist's dream. Dark and imposing, it was a monster of a tree. It was the subject of much Johnson family lore, and of course nightmares. The gnarls, knobs, and weathered notches formed in such a way as to suggest a frowning menace of a face, and a recent lightning strike had managed to bleach jagged, teeth-like markings in a darkened whorl where the Johnsons had already imagined a mouth. The fact that the tree had otherwise gone unscathed was a source of fear for the hearty and hale and otherwise unsuperstitious Johnson boys, who were now forced, under the indomitable will of little Gladiola, to spend time scaling the beast and hammering its branches. There were rumors that some of the smaller trees surrounding it moved, though no one had been able to prove it. Even the oldest among them feared that their construction work would bring dire consequences.

They feared reprisal from Jed more, so the labor-averse Johnson boys went scurrying to and from the tree carrying buckets of old nails, tools, rope, found lumber, and pieces of car, among other ill-conceived construction materials. These furtive actions attracted the attention of Jed Johnson and caused him a great deal of concern. Some of the boys had never even attended a shop class, or a Johnson family shack raising, and so had no experience with construction. He wanted to inspect, shout warnings, offer supervision, but he was wise in the ways of the Johnson younglings, so he knew that he needed to be careful. If Jed were to ask, as he wished, "What the hell are yiz doin!" the boys would clam up or feed him a lie. The boys took after their elders and were absolutely immovable when pressed to rat out their fellow Johnsons. (Another valuable trait for secret government agencies seeking operatives.) Jed opted for subterfuge, and undertook a long and arduous belly crawl, using the cover of the high yellow grass, toward the scene of the crime.

In the course of Jed's serpentine perambulations, he came across a little patch of scorched earth, smelled burnt plastic mingled with the scent of singed human hair. Spokes of twisted metal emerged like some kind of alien antennae from the damaged soil. A cracked flip-flop dangled from them, like a trophy of no value in the hands of an underpaid employee-of-the-month. Jed was perplexed by the scene but could come to no conclusion about it.

As he drew closer to the tree, he could hear the sounds of hammering and sawing, the creaking wood of ladder against tree, whispered requests for tools, and tired little sighs. This was not the rambunctious banter he'd expect from a bunch of Johnson boys Up To No Good. The lone voice of happiness in this uncharacteristically gloomy gang was the serrated-edge laughter of Gladiola Wild Child Johnson.

Jed peered through the grass. The boys assaulted the monster tree while Gladiola spun circles on the ground. Every so often she stopped, giggling, and said, "Dizzy!" then started spinning again. He looked back toward the boys, puzzled.

He waited a few minutes for some revelatory piece of information to reach his ears and was about to call it quits when Gladiola barked, "JP Johnson! Go get me some food and lemonade!"

JP shimmied down the tree and employed a lackluster march to approach Gladiola.

Blowing his overlong blond bangs out of his face, he said, "Come on, Gladiola, give us a break. We're tired!"

Gladiola frowned, holding her dizzy head. "No stopping, or I'll tell Jed!" For emphasis she stomped and little blue sparks rose up from her toes. It was so subtle that Jed thought it might be a trick of the eyes, or blowing dust refracting sunlight. Whatever those specks were, Jed's main concern was that he recognized his cue to enter the scene and Be A Grown-up.

He stood and bellowed, "Tell Jed what?"

Gladiola spun to face him, with a bit too much momentum. She staggered a little when she stopped, but recovered quickly. She smiled and folded her arms in front of her chest. Jed blinked. The girl's hair was sticking straight out from her head, forming a weird, creepy halo.

"I promised not to tell," Gladiola said, smugly.

JP trembled, his brown eyes mournful, and looked at his feet, "We're building Gladiola a treehouse."

Jed put his hands on his hips and puffed up his chest in order to look more imposing. This slight modification of posture had the opposite effect, as it made the dirt stains on his belly more pronounced. "Since when do you boys ever volunteer for projects? Especially ones involving that particular tree?"

A cricket chirped. Everyone shuffled their feet and avoided Jed's gaze.

"Somebody better start talking or you're switching beds with Gladiola tonight."

Jed noticed Gladiola's grin, and that grin was filled with such malice that it scared him. A situation which, in Jed's estimation, was totally ridiculous. Luckily for him, he didn't have to dwell on this tiny bit of emasculated feeling, for little JP stepped forward and offered his shaky voice as sacrifice.

"We did something bad to Gladiola, and now we gotta make up for it."

Donny dropped his hammer. "Not anymore we don't! She told!"

Gladiola cackled and somewhere in the distance a crow echoed the sentiment. "No I didn't."

"No," Donny pouted, "but you hinted, which is the same thing as tellin'."

Gladiola's grin faded and she restated her case, "I didn't tell." This was followed by a graceful little raspberry and an eloquent performance of the Italian gesture meaning, "Fuck you," which caused blue sparks to drift away from her chin.

Jed glowered. "Far as I can tell, nobody told, but it must have been pretty bad for you boys to go after the monster tree."

Little JP burst into tears. He gave up every last detail, each admitted trespass adding another crease to Jed's frown. After JP told his story, he ran away toward the closest shack, ostensibly for comfort.

Jed turned his anger toward the rest of the motley crew. He figured on tall, muscular Donny as the ringleader of this little enterprise, Gladiola the righteous, if particularly mean, victim, and JP a mere pawn in the Johnson family version of chess. An idea formed in his head, and solidified.

"Gladiola, dammit, wipe that smirk off your face!"

She acquiesced, but during the course of Jed's embittered decree, it crept back.

"Okay," Jed said, "Here's what's gonna happen. You boys are all gonna build this damned treehouse in exchange for trying to kill Gladiola. But I'm gonna supervise. That junk you nailed onto that friggin' tree ain't good enough for me to crap on, much less live in. So you little assholes are gonna tear it all down, every last scrap, and you're gonna do it right now."

Donny started to protest. "But—"

"I don't wanna hear a friggin' word out of you!" Jed screamed.

Gladiola giggled.

Jed shot a pained expression her way. "Get back to the house and get cleaned up."

Gladiola shook her head. "Can't."

"And why the hell not?" Jed queried.

Gladiola's expression grew slightly mournful. "Watch." She clapped her hands together rapidly, and those blue sparks sprayed out of her fingertips the way red sparks fly when a welding torch is applied to metal.

Donny jumped back, blue eyes wide with fear, "Jesus H. Christ, Gladiola! Watch it!"

Jed felt something bubbling up inside of him like a furious belch. It burst forth as such hard laughter that he doubled over with it and tears started to form in the corners of his eyes. Donny grumbled, shook his shaven head, and walked lazily toward the tree. When Jed finally recovered he graced Gladiola with his wider-than-the-sky grin and said, "Okay, Sparky, but you come in when it stops. And leave those boys alone. No sense in everyone getting fried."

Jed lumbered away and Gladiola resumed spinning.

***

Jed and the boys managed to build a mighty fine treehouse within a month without loss of life, limb, or too much blood. The tree was surprisingly docile during the construction, growing restive only when the boys packed it in at the end of each day.

The Johnsons forgot to be afraid of the thing.

Situated above the tree's negligible face, the treehouse looked like a weird hat, branches sticking through apertures like aberrant ponytails, making Gladiola the lone bit of lice infiltrating the green coiffure. Speaking of bugs, the tree itself never played host to the things—the one place on the Johnson property that never suffered from the over-population of insects. A boon to Gladiola, but an element of creepiness to the rest of the Johnsons.

The finished product proved to be the most impressive structure built on Johnson family land, with three platforms and a view to the populated areas. Gladiola would be able to see all the activities of the human inhabitants. Jed briefly felt a gnawing suspicion about that until he remembered that Gladiola was only nine years old. Her age raised some concern among the Johnson adult females. Jed gently reminded them that her electrocution occurred when she was theoretically protected by the proximity of adults and an earth-bound living situation. "Besides, lord knows how long she survived all on her ownsome in these here woods." Still, to appease them, he installed a proper drop-down staircase, fitted the place with extra methods of entry and escape, rubber matting for insulation, and even went so far as to bring fire extinguishers onto the Johnson property for the first time in recorded history.

It was time for Jed to gather Gladiola, the boys, and the rest of the Johnsons for a good old-fashioned shack raising party.

Gladiola and JP were the guests of honor, as they were the only two who had never tasted a drop of Johnson moonshine. It was a special brew, fortified with vision-producing herbs, one of its most prized properties. Gladiola stuffed her jug full of marshmallows, which instantly dissolved, while JP drank his straight. When the bonfire was raised and the hallucinations started, Gladiola thought her bogeymen were entertaining, while JP was terrorized and wet his pants again. Soon, all the Johnsons were gathered by the fire, and promises of scary stories about The Tree drew Gladiola. Even though the stone-lined fire pit was twenty feet away from the big tree, she felt she sat in its shadow.

"Not too many years back," said Jed, "Maybe about ten years, there was a Johnson girl here, about seventeen years old, full of life and spunk. Her name was Ambo, on account of none of the kids being able to pronounce her real name. Her favorite thing was to play cops and robbers, even though she was a little old to play pretend. All of us boys were a little bit in love with her."

The kids let out a collective groan. Gladiola farted, poetically.

"Here's to Ambo!" Big George shouted.

"She woulda been a help during my stripper days," Martha said. "Fastest girl alive with a pair of handcuffs."

Jed nodded, "She was a pretty good shot too, if I rightly remember."

Big George grinned, "Old Ambo was the only one who could turn chipmunk huntin' season into a feast. I still got that striped jacket she made me."

"Yeah," said Jed, laughing, "But it don't fit no more."

Gladiola sighed. She was bored with all the grown-up talk. So she picked up her jug of moonshine, grabbed a bucket of cold, greasy fried chicken, and found JP sitting a little away from the fire on a ratty blanket. She snuggled up to the beleaguered and pee-stained JP and started eating her chicken.

"When are they gonna tell the story?" she asked with a mouth full of half-chewed food. The moonshine made the chicken shout, "Don't eat me!" when she bit down, which in Gladiola's estimation made the chicken more tasty.

JP shrugged. Donny came up to them from behind and grabbed a piece of Gladiola's chicken. She threw a bone at him.

Donny smiled and said, "They ain't gonna tell it now. They always start and then end up talking about boring stuff."

JP tugged at Donny's hole-riddled sleeve. "Don't tell it, Donny."

Gladiola raised her jug of moonshine to her lips with both hands and took a long swig. "Don't tell what?"

Donny ruffled JP's hair. "JP doesn't like to be scared. He doesn't want me to tell the story about the big tree."

Gladiola grinned, "I love to be scared."

"Drink some more moonshine, Gladiola. It'll help."

JP shook his head, eyes wide with fear.

Donny began to tell the story. Aided by the moonshine, Gladiola saw, rather than heard the story of The Thing the Tree Did....

Through the hallucinogen-laden ether, Gladiola saw Ambo Johnson standing at the edge of the field, surrounded by high grass. Ambo was tall and imposing, not particularly attractive, but not especially ugly, either. She had intense, almost black eyes and there was something in her gaze that reminded Gladiola of the Magic Man. Gladiola's purple night blended with Ambo's yellow afternoon as the scene from the past merged with the present.

Ambo stared down the tree, holding a sawed-off shotgun, wearing a bow and a quiver full of arrows. The tree groaned and shuddered. It had teardrop-shaped fruit the color of slow-healing bruises hanging from its boughs. They throbbed, condensation glistening, vaguely obscene.

A gang of Johnson kids emerged from the grass behind Ambo, offering protesting shouts, "Don't do it, Ambo! Don't do it."

Gladiola thought she recognized a younger, thinner version of Jed among the group. He seemed a little older than the others, though.

Ambo's gaze stayed on the tree as she said, "Listen here, pudge muffins, ya'll are too scared of that damned tree. Maybe it shakes, and even talks sometimes, but it ain't got feet, and it ain't coming to get you. I'm gonna make sure that's true. Now get behind me."

The kids scattered to points behind Ambo. The tree moaned, its dark green leaves curled around the strange fruit, protectively, as if with intent.

Ambo raised her shotgun, aimed and fired. A large fruit exploded in pieces, scattering seeds and spraying pink and purple pulp into the kids' hair. The tree's creaking sounded like screams.

Satisfied, load spent, and out of ammunition, Ambo put the shotgun down, and reached for her arrows. One by one, her flawless shots divested the tree of fruit. She ignored the shuddering protests of the thing, waiting it out until all noise and movement from the tree subsided. Some of the Johnson kids were crying. Ambo ignored that, too, and started walking toward the tree, eyeing the ground for fallen fruit.

Finding her prize, Ambo smiled, picked it up and waved it in the air. "See! It's fine!" she shouted to the terrorized children. The tree's leaves began to rustle loudly, as if there was a strong wind disturbing them, but there was no wind. Ambo lifted the fruit to her unremarkable lips and sank her teeth into it. The tree shuddered violently and moaned, but she didn't hear it as she chewed.

The kids started shouting, "Look out!"

A dazed expression of bliss slowly filled Ambo's face as she swallowed. It remained even as the tree's largest branch reached out toward her, as some of the Johnson kids screamed and ran and those that stayed behind trembled. Her glowing smile was stubborn, even as the tree spread open in the center, revealing a black, cavernous maw. Ambo's smile faltered only when the branch finally swept her inside and the wood and bark slowly knit back together, with Ambo sealed up behind it. Only one of the Johnsons was left to watch as the tree quaked violently and *swallowed....*

When the story was over, Donny yawned, stretched, and said, "Time to pack it in."

He looked around the dwindling campfire and saw most of the other Johnsons passed out. "Losers," Donny said as he left. Little JP was long gone, having run to the nearest shack in fear.

Gladiola smiled and hugged herself. (She had an overly healthy self-esteem.) She looked up at the treehouse, listened to the tree moan, and ascended her recently hewn staircase. She gazed down at the sleeping Johnsons from her window, and then at the smaller trees nearby. Their branches were spread wide, and in the center of each tree was a large round bump that a scientist would have identified as a mutation, but which to Gladiola were head-shaped, and looked like upturned faces. They gazed up at her and she looked back, smiled, and waved.

Too tired to explore her new home any further, she collapsed on her "bed", which consisted of two sleeping bags sewn together and stuffed with pillows, more pillows, and a pile of blankets. Compared to the dog cage, this was heaven.

But despite her relatively heightened comfort, her sleep was restless and giddy. The tree moaned like the happy mother of a large and dangerous mammal. Lulled by its song, Gladiola dreamt of falling fruit accompanied by a kicking chorus line of singing leaves as Ambo, suited up like the star performer of a 1950s-era synchronized swim team, dove repeatedly into a tar pit. Below the protective boughs of the tree in which Gladiola slept, the Johnsons snored in teeth-grinding harmony.

At the edge of the field, surveying this quaint scene, was a tall man in a dark red coat. Slow, ponderous steps caused a hush to fall over the crooning crickets. He raised his arms like a conductor and guided the syncopated snores of the Johnsons to a melodious noise, the likes of which the world would never want foisted upon itself, but which pleased the Magic Man. The William Tell Overture as performed by a symphony of vibrating nostrils was somewhat anticlimactic.

The woman dogging the Magic Man's steps did not share his taste for music, though she did share his dark hair, sensual looks, and penchant for red clothing. Her red velvet gown fluttered gracefully around her body as she approached. She pursed her lips, then raised a finger, and the snoring Johnsons suddenly switched gears and began a rendition of Dueling Banjos that was utterly bowel-shaking.

The Magic Man rested his elaborately cuffed hands on his hips and said, "Minerva, you always have to bring things to the gutter, don't you?"

Minerva's eyes glittered, "That's the way you like it, Devlin."

Devlin smirked in response and offered his arm to the lady. "You still know how to push my buttons, sister."

He guided her toward the tree in which Gladiola slept. Goosebumps rose at the back of Minerva's neck and she shivered. "Ooooo, Devlin, I recognize this tree."

Devlin smiled, "Yes."

Behind them, the Johnsons' tuneful snores degenerated into the usual rhythms associated with human breathing, occluded and otherwise. Cricket song returned to the field beyond.

As they reached the bottom of the tree, Minerva raised a bell-sleeved arm and snapped her well-manicured fingers. The drop-down staircase gently lowered itself.

Devlin pried a mostly full bottle of moonshine from the fingers of the nearest sleeping Johnson, wiped the lip of the jug and took a drink.

Minerva turned to him, "Now who is the one in the gutter?"

"This is quality stuff, and it's charmingly illegal."

The pair ascended the staircase and gained entrance to Gladiola's boudoir. Finding nowhere to sit, Minerva levitated, suspended halfway between the floor and the ceiling. Her shapely legs were folded into a perfect lotus position that would have made Buddha envious. She looked down at the sleeping Gladiola, the nearly empty jug of moonshine next to a depleted bag of marshmallows situated near the child's head.

"This is the oracle maker?" Minerva asked skeptically.

"She doesn't look like much, does she?" Devlin responded.

"No," Minerva said flatly, closing her eyes meditatively.

"I know," Devlin said quietly, "but I'm telling you this kid has a good chance of succeeding."

Minerva opened her eyes. "I'm just not convinced she was worth the magic utensils. What if it's gone? She's a nine-year-old, Devlin."

Devlin shrugged. "We can always make more silverware."

"But it was so hard and it took such a long time," Minerva whined.

Devlin's tone became sharp. "We need an oracle, sister, so we don't keep wasting our time on schemes which will come to naught."

Minerva smiled apologetically and unfolded her legs. "I know that, Devlin. I just wish we already had one so that we could tell which one of our oracle-making schemes will work. And I'm feeling a bit lazy. The banshees of Ireland were exhausting."

Devlin grinned and reached out a hand to caress the sleek curve of his sister's hip, "But worth it. Banshees make the best athletic trainers."

Gladiola stirred.

"Don't wake her up!" Minerva hissed. "Find the silverware!"

Devlin bowed, then knelt over Gladiola and rubbed his hands together. He breathed on them. The condensation mixed with particles in the air created an alchemical golden bubble which he then cast over the sleeping Gladiola. It stretched to accommodate her whole body.

Minerva smiled and knelt beside Devlin, whispering, "I love it when you do this trick."

Devlin thrilled at the compliment, but did not allow his pleasure to divert him from his task. The bubble formed a liquid screen, with random swirling whorls of color.

"Let me see your memories, little girl," Devlin whispered.

Gladiola yawned, and as she rolled over, a puff of white cloud came out of her ear. The cloud spread out, shifted shapes and danced erratically, then finally solidified into a discernible recording of her recent past.

Scanning the memories for signs of the missing silverware, Devlin and Minerva found it difficult not to laugh out loud at the lightning incident. There were hazy depictions of Gladiola making use of the fork to cook meat, and the spoon to melt ice, but they found nothing that revealed the current location of the utensils. The siblings concluded that the silverware had to be in the hands of one of the Johnsons.

Neither Devlin nor Minerva could raise a malevolent finger against the clan.

The Johnsons and the Du Mauvais siblings had crossed metaphysical paths only once before during the siblings' six hundred years of existence. The present generation of Johnsons had no inkling of that ancient family story, other than a vague idea that once upon a time there had been a famous Johnson witch capable of healing everything from broken bones to thumbscrew scars. Devlin and Minerva du Mauvais were the only ones who knew the whole sordid tale, and that was only because they had been there, circa 1692.

In that year, the Johnson family were not nearly as insular a clan, less incestuous, and, oddly, more hygienic. The Johnson farm was clean and well-tended, known for the quality of livestock, the fineness of their horses, the remarkably large size of their chickens' eggs, and the beauty of their garden. The clan was never seen at church, a particularly dangerous set of circumstances in that year of North American history; but because the property lay between the borders of two towns, each congregation assumed the Johnsons attended the others' services.

Felicity Johnson was the matriarch of the family. At forty-three, she was youthful-looking for a woman of her age, and possessed most of her natural teeth, a rare quality. Well-versed in the arts of herbal medicine, the townsfolk on both sides of the Johnson family sprawl paid visits to Felicity for draughts, poultices, and ampules for those laid low by illness. Her remedies worked without fail and the people trusted her implicitly. The Johnsons were well thought of until the day that the dark and handsome Frenchman, Devlin du Mauvais, arrived with his mysterious widowed sister, Minerva.

Gossip circulated among the local population that Mssr. du Mauvais had brought his sister to America for an adventure, to heighten her spirits after the demise of her late husband. In reality, the sibling sorcerers were looking for new magic, and Minerva was perpetually veiled only because of a failed shape-shifting experiment involving snakes. Her face was a hot mess of scales. They'd stopped in Varksnort Haven, drawn by the pleasant weather, the scent on the wind of pigs to the slaughter, and the cries of hanging witches in its neighboring towns. Finally they chose to stop there because they could sense Felicity Johnson's power.

The kitchen witch was strong, but not so strong as to be capable of conquering the du Mauvais. Felicity was intended to be a light snack before they moved on to follow the trail of darker creatures in the New World. But how to get what they wanted of her? It was up to Devlin to set and bait the trap, as Minerva had to remain veiled and hidden. She hated being held back by her temporary deformity, but still thought the failed experiment was worth it, especially the look on the Notromanian snake handler's face just before she swallowed him whole. So it was that Devlin stoically attended the paint-drying religious services in the towns on either side of Johnson land, merely to inform the inhabitants of each place that he had never seen the Johnsons at either church. This social espionage raised eyebrows, but not suspicions. At least, not enough suspicion to successfully exploit the witch-hunting craze that had just begun to hit the colonies. Even this puritanical little community needed more ammunition.

Devlin and Minerva moved on to phase two, which involved Minerva's blazing talent for hexes. Devlin gathered the names of children recently treated by Felicity Johnson's herbs and then fed them to Minerva's boiling cauldron. Immediately, all of those children fell ill; some even died, succumbing to sickness both unidentifiable and otherworldly. Speculation and rumor begat resentment and accusation, paving Felicity Johnson's way to her Meeting with an Unfortunate End.

The set for the final scene in Felicity's life comprised a tree, an angry mob, beautiful blue skies, circling crows, the opulent black carriage of the du Mauvais, and its notorious passengers.

If the angry mob felt that a hanging was an all-too-brief and anticlimactic sentence for Felicity Johnson, the soon-to-be-deceased had quite the opposite experience. Everything slowed down, and the reluctant rise up the ladder to the waiting noose lasted an eternity until at long, interminable last she stood to face the crowd.

Felicity's slow-motion world pulled its focus in on the du Mauvais horses, beasts so black they were almost blue. They seemed large and demonic to Felicity, with a red stain of malice in their equine eyes, and horns sprouting where they should not. The carriage itself defied logic, shining where it should have been matte, like an egregiously abused piece of suede.

Devlin du Mauvais stood just beside the carriage door, lounging against it with a smile on his face, while the veiled Minerva remained inside. Uneasy enough about her imminent death, Felicity felt an alarm even greater, gazing out at Devlin while the preacher who marched her toward death shouted weak justifications for the hanging at the mob. Her eyes roamed the crowd wildly, seeking something familiar and comforting for her last moment of existence, but her attention was drawn back to the du Mauvais. Felicity locked eyes with Devlin and she suddenly understood that he was no ordinary Frenchman, but rather a practitioner of the dark arts who meant her family harm. She raised her chin defiantly and thought, *though my death be inevitable, the metaphysical rape of the Johnson family is not.*

Felicity closed her eyes and focused all her energy on the tree from which she was about to swing. She pictured herself as the tree, strong and sturdy, surviving against the climate, against the ages, drawing strength from the earth through her roots, gaining sustenance from the sun through her leaves and branches.

The earth shook. The skies darkened. Felicity's whole body began to glow as she emitted an eerie, long-sustained moan. It grew louder, into a cry for protection of the Johnson family against the du Mauvais, the summoning of a curse.

The crowd went silent, the shaking ground kicked the ladder from beneath Felicity's feet, and she hung, choking, larynx crushed by her own weight against the rope. Even as she died, her strange cries echoed across the field. At the moment of expiration, there was a blinding flash, the crowd fled, and Felicity was gone. Vanished, body and soul.

Devlin leapt into the carriage, covering his eyes, blinded and foiled. He and Minerva were alone among the mob in understanding precisely what had just transpired. Not only had Felicity Johnson successfully foiled the most powerful pair of sorcerers to walk the earth in over five hundred years, she had also *merged* with the tree. And as any sorcerer worth his or her salt could tell you, magic performed at the moment of death was absolutely undoable. The tree would never be felled, and Felicity was now more powerful than Devlin and Minerva together.

The problem this created for the du Mauvais as they moved on to their next misadventure was this: above all things they desired an oracle of their own. They wanted an oracle to help them predict the outcome of their magical experiments, to tell them which of their plans were likely to be successful. Though they had the power to live indefinitely, plans, schemes, and new magical techniques took a lot of time to develop, and with an oracle to tell them in advance which of these were not likely to bear fruit, they could waste less time and enjoy an increase in skill and power much more quickly. The du Mauvais hated to admit this, but for every fifty lengthy experiments, only one was successful.

The magical power which coursed through the Johnsons' veins made them ideal candidates to become oracles, and increased the likelihood of success. Felicity's death was supposed to make the rest of the family vulnerable. If the matriarch had no opportunity to pass on her knowledge, to teach the others how to use their magic, then the Johnsons would be defenseless. But Felicity was still around to protect them. If the du Mauvais were ever to succeed, they needed an intermediary.

And now, three hundred years later, they'd finally found one; but she was only nine, and the fact that she now slept amid Felicity's protective boughs made things a little sticky, whether it was tree-tapping season or not.

Disappointed, Devlin released Gladiola from the bubble, rueing the day of the event which prevented him from interfering with the Johnsons directly.

As if sensing Devlin's need for comfort, Minerva rubbed his bottom. "Devlin, the silverware. We need to get it back."

Devlin sighed. "Of course." He leaned in to whisper into Gladiola's ear. "It is time I shared with you my proper name, Gladiola. It is a name of power, a name of—"

Minerva kicked at the bottom of his shoe. "Don't be so theatrical."

Devlin cleared his throat, "My name is Devlin du Mauvais, and I need my silverware back." He backed away and stood up, facing Minerva. "Was that straightforward enough for you?"

Minerva planted a long, tongue-swishing kiss on her brother. He took that as a yes.

The tree began to moan and shake.

"Felicity knows we're here," Minerva said, then dove out of the nearest treehouse window. Devlin followed her lead.

***

Dawn slowly reclaimed the Johnson sprawl, reviving its moonshine-saturated inhabitants. If some of the clan did not respond to the rapidly increasing light, there were birds to wake them with sound. Woodpeckers knocked rapidly against nearby trees, doves cooed, and crows cawed. Jed and Martha were careful to bang dishes together as they cleaned up the little campsite. Big George restarted the fire, adding his own noise to the wake-up call as the effort of moving around and bending to his task caused him to grunt.

A good shack raising always included a campfire breakfast. It was up to Jed and Martha to gather the supplies for the feast while the others slowly rolled themselves to wakefulness and went to their respective toilettes to perform varying degrees of self-maintenance. On this auspicious morning, the process mostly involved throwing up and gargling. The ratio of Johnsons who actually bothered to brush their teeth to those who didn't was two to one. (Jed was in the percentage that underwent this arduous ritual, he had to protect his impressive grin.) Big George didn't concern himself with such matters that morning, as he was graced with an iron constitution excluding him from the experience of the moonshine hangover, and knew that as cook he would wind up greasier than a hog in a fire pit regardless of how clean he got before he started.

Jed and Martha arrived back at the campfire with piles of food. Potatoes as big as cats, sausage links the size of Gladiola's forearm, onions as pungent as patchouli oil on an unwashed hippie, eggs comparable to JP's head, and pancake batter as smooth as Devlin du Mauvais' waxed and wicked ass.

The scent of cooking wafted up into the treehouse and startled Gladiola awake, so great was her hunger. As she stood and stretched, Felicity's leaves unfurled. Had anyone bothered to look up, they might have thought the tree's activity was a bit like that of a cat waking up after a nap, fur lifting and then relaxing. Gladiola climbed down the staircase, hair messed, wrapped in a tattered blanket that trailed a bit behind her as she walked. She thought she caught glimpses of saplings walking around along the edge of the woods, faces turned toward the Johnsons.

Mouth watering, she sat near the fire, watching Big George and Jed masterfully flip the flapjacks, tong the taters, and fry the omelets. Gladiola was first in line for pancakes and mystery syrup. As soon as Jed handed her the eating utensils required for the consumption of such a feast, Gladiola was overwhelmed with longing for her wooden fork and spoon. She tugged on Jed's jeans.

"Where's my silverware?" she demanded.

Jed raised eyebrows that were dangerously close to becoming eyebrow. "You still half asleep, Gladiola? I just gave you some."

"No," she answered with a pout. "*My* silverware. The set I came with."

Jed was confused until he recalled the set of red wood utensils he had stashed in a special box near his bed. He smiled, "I'll get 'em for ya right after breakfast."

Gladiola calmed and said, "Okay."

Jed was pleased, seeing her quiet acceptance of this as an Overall Improvement of Behavior. It confirmed for him that by taking Gladiola in, he had Done the Right Thing.

Gladiola settled herself on the ground to devour her breakfast.

***

Right after breakfast, as promised, Jed delivered the magic utensils unto the expectant Gladiola. They had gathered a little dust since she had last grasped them with her grubby hands, but they had not suffered any damage. Her face beamed, she hugged Jed's knees as he laughed and patted her head. He was puzzled, but Gladiola was happy, positively charming, and that was enough to widen his grin and make his eyes shine.

Gladiola ran off into the high grass and squatted, waiting. Something moved through the grass and she quietly raised the fork, wielding it like a warrior's javelin. Jed watched as she sat in that position for over a minute. He blinked when she swiftly stabbed the fork into something with the precision of a practiced hunter. An image came to mind of Little Red Riding Hood, reversing her own story and eating the Big Bad Wolf.

His smile disappeared and his brows leapt to meet his hairline as the smell of cooking meat wafted toward him, mingling with the smells of the fire. A puff of smoke and steam drifted up from the spot where Gladiola had jabbed the fork. She stood, bearing with her the fork, which in turn bore the weight of a freshly baked grouse. She giggled and walked proudly over to Jed, the way a child approaches a parent when she is about to say, "Watch what I can do!"

She ripped off a perfectly de-feathered wing and offered it to Jed. "Try some!"

He accepted the gift wordlessly and watched Gladiola as she skipped back into the field. Jed was bereft of coherent thought.

Big George walked up behind him, "Hey Jed! You're burning the flapjacks!"

Jed swallowed and pointed to the grass parted by the wake of Gladiola's exit. "Did you see that?"

George blinked. "See what?"

"Gladiola. She—"

George patted Jed on the back, "That girl's a pip. She's coming along though, Big Daddy. Didn't even try to bite anyone last night. Now come on, we gotta finish feeding the other Johnsons afore we can eat."

Jed docilely followed Big George back to the campfire.

***

Summer progressed, and Gladiola went hunting with her fork every day. Donny and Little JP became her hunting buddies. She swore the boys to secrecy about their hunting, somehow knowing in the back of her mind that the Magic Man would not be happy with any indiscretion regarding the utensils. The wily trio managed to keep it secret for quite a while. Gladiola had somehow found Ambo's old quiver and took to carrying the utensils in it everywhere she went. She never took it off except to bathe. Donny and Gladiola played the hunters, using JP as bait. Over the summer months Donny turned thirteen, and the constant supply of fresh protein from lean meat helped him grow even taller and more muscular.

It wasn't until late August that Gladiola, Donny, and JP got themselves into a heap of trouble. They were in

Gladiola's treehouse, decorating it with the bleached bones of their kills. Felicity was being unusually noisy, because unbeknownst to Gladiola, Devlin and Minerva du Mauvais were approaching in order to try and reclaim what was theirs. As they drew nearer, the tree began to shake. Gladiola was used to it and ignored Felicity, even though Donny and JP were careful to stay still in the center of the treehouse. She'd made bone wind chimes to hang in Felicity's branches and climbed out on one of the sturdier boughs to hang them.

She saw Devlin and Minerva approaching from the woods and recognized them, smiled, and waved. Felicity heaved violently and Gladiola fell. Donny and JP rushed out to the window even as the floor pitched and rolled like a ship caught in a storm. They too, pitched forward. All three screamed. As they fell, Felicity swept a gigantic branch forward and once more opened her great big mouth, swallowing Gladiola, Donny, and JP whole. Devlin and Minerva howled.

Devlin and Minerva felt dejected as Felicity closed herself up again. They swore that as the seam sealed, the tree smiled triumphantly at them.

Devlin looked at Minerva apologetically. "I'm sorry, dear sister. Your instincts were right. I should never have started this silly plan."

Minerva sighed and drew closer. She pushed a shiny black tendril of hair back behind his ear and kissed his cheek. "We've been without an oracle all these years, Devlin. We can wait. Time is on our side. And you are forgetting that our experiments, even when they fail, always prove useful. Something productive will come of this. You'll see."

Devlin reached for the hand caressing his face and kissed its soft palm. "I'm sure you are right, dear sister."

***

Gladiola, JP and Donny were dumped into a sticky well of tree sap, Felicity's bowels widened by Ambo's long-ago passage. Like heavy sediment, the three children sifted slowly to the bottom of the tree, gulping lungfuls of hot, heavy air whenever they came upon a bubble. It was only a matter of hours before they found the bottom of Felicity's digestive tract.

There was a great sucking sound and they were pulled downward, the pressure stretching their flailing limbs uncomfortably, each convinced that this was The End. Gladiola fought her pain and the slow momentum to reach into the quiver for the spoon. As she pulled it out, she heard the groans of Felicity muffled and distorted by the syrup. Gladiola gritted her teeth and banged the spoon, in slow motion, against a dense mass of coagulating syrup within reach. It rang like a bell and emitted a short burst of red-gold light. The liquid suspending the children lost its viscosity, Felicity let out a complaining whine, and the contents of the great tree's bowels were flushed out through an opening in the center of her expansive roots.

One might assume that the children were drowned by the flood of weird soup created by the contact of Gladiola's broth-making spoon with the glob of tree sap; or that they were perhaps crushed beneath the tree, trapped by impacted dirt, clay, and rocks. But what lay on the other side of Felicity's wood-lined asshole was not what anyone would expect to find. There was, instead, a narrow, gravel-lined passage heading downward on a soft incline. Rivulets of tree by-product ran along the path, and the way was made slippery as a symptom of Felicity's unwanted diuretic. Though the air was fetid and stank of hot sucre, the children rejoiced. Gladiola, JP, and Donny jumped up and down in excitement, and joined together in an impulsive group hug—a mistake, since they spent the next five minutes trying to get unstuck from each other.

Once that was accomplished, Gladiola checked to make sure that her fork was still inside her gooey quiver. She found it, and rather than returning the spoon to join its partner, she took out the fork and held them both in front of her as she led the way down. The pass was dark, so she made JP hold onto her shoulder, and Donny held onto JP, creating a human chain. They muddled their way through slowly, stumbling on the rocks, joy fading along the way.

Finally, when they thought that their legs would fail them, they lurched forward into a huge cave. Moisture appeared on the walls, streaks of old mineral deposits glistened in the light thrown by torches that were anchored to the walls by iron sconces. In contrast to that, thickly insulated cables lay strewn to one side of the cave, leading to the opposite side where an arched entrance to another passageway could be seen. Green light spilled out onto the floor from that hallway.

Gladiola and JP looked at each other, then glanced behind them. Donny was no longer with them.

"Where's Donny?" JP asked, his voice small and frightened.

A shadow fell across them and they turned to see a woman smiling at them.

"I see you've found my quiver, little one," the woman said.

Gladiola squinted at the figure as she brandished her fork.

"Don't worry about your friend. I will see that he's safe," the woman said. "Although, I promise you won't remember any of this."

JP whimpered.

"Who are you?" Gladiola demanded.

The woman smiled again. "Don't you recognize me, children? I'm Ambo."

She approached Gladiola and JP. It wasn't until she was almost on top of them that Gladiola noticed Ambo held a small brown bottle. The top of that bottle was covered by a white cloth.

Gladiola lunged at Ambo with her fork, but Ambo easily side-stepped the fork. She grabbed Gladiola's wrist, forcing her to drop the utensil and covered the girl's face with the cloth. The last thing Gladiola remembered, was JP calling out, "No!"

***

Devlin and Minerva were frolicking naked in the woods, doing everything they could to distract themselves from their disappointment in Gladiola, when they heard the summons. There was a timorous little stream nearby. Water was the best medium in nature for the transmission of messages, so Devlin and Minerva availed themselves of it, using a rock with a natural hollow to make a scrying pool.

Devlin waved his hands over the water, and an annoyingly smug young woman's face appeared.

Minerva rankled, "Who are you?"

The young woman smiled, "Well, I'm glad to see the du Mauvais haven't lost their manners." Her smile faded to a grim line of seriousness. "Who I am is of no importance. But what I happen to possess at the moment, well, that's another story."

Devlin and Minerva looked at each other, perplexed. They could tell that the young woman was no sorceress, and yet she had been able to locate them. The woman stepped aside to reveal the sleeping, angelic faces of JP and Gladiola.

Devlin gasped. Minerva threw up her hands.

The young woman smiled. "And if I have them, then you must know what else I have."

"But how—" Devlin started.

Ambo's eyes glittered. "Let's just say that Felicity is a very good teacher."

Devlin became all business. "You have a proposal."

Ambo nodded. "I will set the children free. Their memories of what occurred after falling into the tree have been erased. You will not be able to find me. I have your tools. I'm assuming you want those returned to you?"

Minerva shouted, "Of course we want them back!"

Devlin said, "Be quiet, Minerva!" He turned back to face Ambo. "Yes I want them back."

"I shall return them to you directly in exchange for this. You will cease and desist all plans against the Johnsons through any intermediary agent. You will not return for at least fifty years."

Devlin took a moment to think about it. Restrictions, unless placed in a sexual context, annoyed him, but what was fifty years to a being such as himself?

"Agreed."

"Devlin!" Minerva protested.

"Well then," said Ambo. "Here you are."

Ambo's hand reached up through the water, holding the fork and spoon. Minerva snatched them and asked, "If you have no magic of your own, how are you doing this?"

Ambo winked, "Felicity is more alive and aware than you think. Take care."

Her image blinked out, leaving behind an ordinary clouded pool.

Minerva smacked the back of Devlin's head. "That silverware was not worth fifty years of restrictions!"

Devlin shrugged, "You were the one who didn't feel like making another set of magic utensils."

Minerva pouted.

***

Gladiola and JP woke up just behind the tree-line. It was daylight, early morning judging by the harshness of the sun.

JP rubbed his eyes and said, "Where's Donny?"

Gladiola stretched and said, "Where are my things?" Alarmed, she stood up and stomped her feet. "Where are my things?"

"Gladiola! Look at your clothes," JP let out a garbled shout.

Gladiola looked down at herself and saw that her dress was stained with something red. She screamed.

JP whispered, "What happened to us down there?"

She shook her head, eyes wide and noticed that JP's clothes were also marked with red smears.

At that moment, Jed came rushing toward them through a clump of bushes. (Which was unnecessary, there was plenty of space on either side.)

"Where in the hell have you two been!" he howled, his toothsome mouth full of rage.

Gladiola was too happy to see Jed to be scared of his anger. She ran toward him and threw her arms around his legs. With a sob in her voice, she cried out, "Daddy!"

This was the first time Gladiola called Jed Daddy. It stunned him and tugged at his heart strings more than a smidge. He kept his anger and frustration contained, knowing that he was only angry because he was scared for them. But he had a new worry. What could possibly have been so terrible to make the courageous, if naughty, Gladiola Johnson cry as she was doing now on his shoulder?

JP sat on the ground shaking, staring woefully. Still cradling the weeping Gladiola's head against his shoulder, Jed asked, "JP? What happened?"

The little boy shook his head, "Don't know."

Eyes wide, heart skipping a few beats, Jed asked, "Where's Donny?"

JP's only answer was to pull his knees up to his chest and press his forehead to them. This time, he did not wet himself, he only wept.

Jed very carefully set Gladiola back on the ground and turned his attention to the ground. No evidence of blood, and there weren't any tracks that might have belonged to Donny. Still, the red stains on both of the kids' clothes gave him pause. The Johnsons were guilty of many petty crimes, but never murder. Not murder. Was it possible that these two tiny children were capable? Maybe Gladiola, but—no. Jed knew in his gut that was not what had happened. He was no homicide detective, but he knew what it looked like. And the kids were too shaken to talk. He had to act fast to protect them.

His voice became very low and serious. "JP. Gladiola. Look at me."

They reluctantly did as they were told, their tiny faces gray and morose.

Jed inhaled deeply, "Now listen to me, very carefully. Go to the treehouse. Get cleaned up. Gladiola, you have to burn that dress. Donny fell down an old mine shaft, and you were lost. Do you understand? It wasn't your fault. Now say it back to me."

Gladiola said, "Donny fell down an old mine shaft."

"We were lost," JP added weakly.

"Good, now go."

The two children ran clumsily toward the treehouse, leaving Jed to consider the scene. He smelled sugar and burnt wood. The kids were too traumatized, they couldn't remember. Jed had never seen Gladiola scared by anything. He hoped they'd never remember, for their sake as well as his own.

***

Back at the treehouse, JP stared at the floor while Gladiola changed her clothes and got cleaned up. She burned the dress in a large ceramic bowl.

Through the wafting smoke, she stared at JP and said, "I want to be a normal kid."

Returning Gladiola's gaze, JP said, "Ain't no such thing."

"But you're a normal kid, JP," Gladiola approached and grabbed his hand, eyes wide and pleading. "Teach me how."

JP shrugged. "Okay."

***

Gladiola squirmed and moaned while she slept. Felicity creaked a comforting lullaby, but it didn't work. Calm only came when Gladiola saw Devlin and Minerva smiling down at her.

"You don't remember, do you?" asked Minerva.

"No," answered a mournful Gladiola.

"Maybe it's for the best," Devlin added, though Gladiola could tell he didn't believe that.

Gladiola struggled with herself, wanting to be with Devlin and Minerva, but wanting something else that would make it impossible.

"Gladiola, what does your heart desire?" Minerva whispered.

"I want to be normal," she said.

Devlin and Minerva exchanged looks, communicating something that Gladiola could not hear.

Devlin kissed Gladiola's brow. "You shall have that, then. Until you are grown. You want the fork and the spoon back, too, don't you?"

"Yes!" cried Gladiola.

"When you are grown, you will have your own child, and name him Andrew Johnson. You will give that child to me, we will make him a great oracle, and then I will show you how to make your own fork and spoon."

Devlin and Minerva looked at each other and smiled, their features warping, eyes turning black as coals, their faces sprouting bony spurs. Gladiola whimpered.

"You will do this Gladiola," they said in unison, "or there will be consequences."

Gladiola's voice shook, "But can I still be normal?"

"Until the time comes, yes," Devlin said.

"Don't forget your promise," Minerva added. She snapped her fingers, and she and Devlin vanished.

Later that night, Gladiola received another visitation, which woke her from troubled sleep. Felicity was silent as JP crawled onto the pile of pillows next to Gladiola. He wrapped a clammy hand around hers and said, "Can I stay with you Gladiola? I can't sleep."

"Bad dreams," she said, sleepily turning toward him, throwing her arm around him.

"Yes," answered JP, burrowing further into the blankets.

The two children squirmed, looking for a comfortable position, until finally they settled on fetal, with Gladiola behind JP, her arm thrown protectively over his torso.

Together they drifted off to a deep, dreamless sleep. Felicity joined them.

Acknowledgements

Well, no book comes to be in the world without a lot of support for the author. This short story collection owes a debt of thanks to a long list of folks. The stories within, some of which have been published elsewhere, would never have reached that status if not for the CLAW critique group in State College, PA and the group of critiquers from the Zoetrope boards. I'd like to particularly thank some of the editors I have sold work to over the years. Dario Ciriello, Gregory Miller, Isabelle Rose and Jessica A. Weiss. Dario gets another thanks for being gracious enough to write the introduction to this collection. Cover art by Alice Teeple makes me giddy with joy.

For beta reads and general writing support, I'd like to thank Devon Miller, Che Gilson, Juliette Wade, Jennifer and Kent Rauch, aka Rune Skelley, Kristen Tsetsi, and RJ Keller. Mark Boltz-Robinson totally wins at vocal support for my work via internet. If you see him, give him a yam, but don't ask why…

Thanks to my family, blood and chosen, for believing in this thing I do.

And of course, thank you, dear reader.

www.ingramcontent.com/pod-product-compliance
Lightning Source LLC
Chambersburg PA
CBHW060423130626
46555CB00005B/2189